# TAKEN BY THE MANBEAST

LEGENDS OF BRAEYORK
BOOK TWO

MORGAN RUSH

# DOWNLOAD YOUR FREE BOOK!

## LOVE LESSONS, (SEQUEL TO SOLD TO THE KING)

**Love Lessons is the steamy mini-sequel to *Sold to the King*, Book 1 of the *Legends of Braeyork* series.**

It is free for all my subscribers!

And if you follow me as a subscriber, you'll also learn more about the characters and their juicy secrets, explore maps of the Braeyork Dominion and be the first to know about hot new books in the *Legends of Braeyork* series.

**Get your free copy of Love Lessons**

Already a subscriber? Download Love Lessons here.

**Follow me and enjoy the *Rush!***

*Morgan*

# PROLOGUE

I could not have imagined a worse fate than being forced to service the commander of the King's Elite Guards in preparation for being sent to the royal harem of concubines.

But would I be any better off if I was taken by a wild half-man, half-wolf creature?

How would I be treated by a towering manbeast covered in white hair with fangs protruding from his slobbering mouth?

Yes, I was a half-thing too – more Fae than human. I was still pure and innocent in the ways of men, an orphan raised by my grandfather in this sleepy, remote part of the Braeyork Dominion.

And I knew what men wanted when they stared at me. No matter what I wore, I could not disguise my full figure from their leering eyes. Was it only a matter of time before my innocence was ripped from me?

But when the inner thoughts of the manbeast's monstrous desire filled my mind through some kind of psychic connection to each other, would I fight him too?

Or would he be the one who ultimately would save me?

# 1

## FLAME

I probably should have known that being the only woman in a pub overflowing with strong ale and even stronger intoxicated soldiers would lead to trouble. As the conversations grew increasingly raunchy and the supply of my grandfather's hearty Dunfeld ale began to dwindle, trouble certainly seemed about to spill over.

"You a maiden yet, wench? How old are you, girl?"

I dropped an overflowing tankard of dark ale on the table of the uniformed man posing the question. His drunk companions grunted, leering at me with a mouthful of filthy teeth.

I glared at the questioner. Captain Mason Hawke, the odorous commander of the King's cavalry, had arrived late last night. Beads of sweat covered my forehead. My thin blouse, drenched from the spray of pouring and serving hundreds of rounds of foaming beer, clung to me like a second skin. The soaked material barely hid the fullness of my breasts and my dark nipples from a room full of wanton eyes.

"None of your business, sir," I snorted.

I dared not show an ounce of weakness. If I let him know I had just turned twenty or lost my composure and revealed the secret of my true Fae nature, the morning would end even worse than the last two hours of being ogled and pawed by the rowdy mob of men in my grandfather's tiny establishment. The Painted Owl was the only inn and pub in the remote village of Dunfeld.

Despite my terse response, Captain Hawke smiled as he lifted his glass and drank deeply, draining half of the ale before setting it down, wiping his lips, and releasing a foul belch.

"You're Flame. Right?"

He inspected me up and down, nodding his head and licking his lips like a slobbering dog. "And are you a *natural* ginger?" he laughed, glancing at the other two dimwitted officers sitting with him.

One reached over and grabbed my arm.

"Ginger all over?" Captain Hawke sneered as the man tightened his grip around my wrist. "Maybe you should show us more, girl, so we don't have to be left wondering when we dream about you alone in our bunks tonight with only our hand to give us... *comfort*."

The grinning officer was hurting me as he twisted my wrist, forcing my arm behind me.

"Leave her alone!"

The commanding tone of my grandfather Omar broke the officer's hold. Omar stepped closer, nodding for me to return to the bar. I took a step back, but the hand of Captain reached for my arm and held it firmly.

"Stay with me, Ginger," he laughed, rising to face my grandfather.

Both were imposing men. Only Omar's grey hair and beard hinted at a man of sixty. Captain Hawke belched again and curled his thin purple lips.

"She somethin' to you?" Hawke sneered. "My little Miss Ginger?"

"My granddaughter," Omar snarled. "Let her go. My ale's running low. It's time for you and your men to leave."

I glanced around the room, which had grown quiet. Unshaven and dishevelled soldiers watched the drama with leering grins. All that is, except for one tall groomed soldier, sitting alone at the far corner table. His penetrating eyes caught mine.

*Don't worry. I'm here.*

The words filled my mind as if someone was talking to me. The striking dark-eyed man in the corner nodded.

The Captain yanked my arm and scowled at my grandfather. "I'll leave when you pay the Crown Tithes and taxes we came here to collect. One gold coin for your inn and one hundred bushels of wheat for the Crown farmlands the King graciously allows you to till for him."

"Are you insane?" my grandfather retorted. "The Painted Owl barely makes a dozen copper pennies. And last year, we struggled to pay fifty bushels in rent."

The Captain locked his arm around my waist. "King Shane has doubled the Crown Tithes, sir. And all inns and pubs in Braeyork now pay a gold coin tax if they wish to sell their ale."

"I can't pay that!" Omar cried. "I have no gold coins. And a hundred bushels of wheat? We won't have enough left to live on. We'll starve."

Captain Hawke twisted my arm around and then yanked me to him. His breath stank of belched ale. He pressed his pocked face to mine. Without looking away, he grinned.

"I can reduce the rent if we can make a deal for Ginger here. The King's third-wife was beheaded last week for insubordination, and his stock of fuck dolls runs low."

"Never!" my grandfather shouted, trying to grab me away from Captain Hawke.

The two officers sitting at the table jumped up and restrained my grandfather, pushing him to the floor. One of them pressed his head to the floor under the sole of a heavy black boot.

"Nice view, Omar?" the Captain chuckled. "Why don't we make a deal?" He squeezed my chin and started to kiss me, trying to snake his thick tongue through my clenched teeth.

I gasped when he groped one of my breasts, allowing his tongue to worm into my mouth while he kneaded the mass of my tit firmly in his hand. The shock of his lewd action was made sicker by his swine-like grunting.

I tried to free myself, but the Captain held his other hand around my stomach as he fondled my breast. He ground his loins into my backside while the men in the pub cheered him on.

Burning with rage, I imagined getting my hands around his neck. I wanted to hurt him like he was hurting me—choke the very life out of this disgusting pig.

I closed my eyes, picturing myself strangling this animal to death as he pulled his tongue out and began slobbering kisses around my jaw and neck.

## 2

## THERON

How much more of this could I take without hating myself for watching? Watching and doing nothing to stop the filthy bastard.

Until now, I had managed to keep a low profile as a member of the Calvary, the King's elite Guard. I kept my emotions in check, fearful of the consequences of letting the beast within me take control should I give in to constant rage as I reluctantly followed the orders of Captain Mason Hawke.

But watching him molest this young woman was the final straw.

Walking into the inn this morning with the rest of the men, I couldn't help but stare at her as if I had been struck by a thunderbolt from the gods.

*Flame.*

Her name suited her perfectly. The color of her long hair reminded me of a glowing sunset, casting waves of burning orange and fiery red as far as the eye could see.

Her mysterious olive-shaped eyes, when they caught mine just now, were impossibly curious and passionate – flecks of forest green surrounded by a pool of turquoise. But there was more, something mysterious and hidden about this woman.

And try as I might, I could not help but lust after the swell of her breasts and the curves of her wide hips revealed so clearly in her soaked clothing.

I knew every man in this crowded pub wanted exactly the same as me – to see her naked, to fuck, and ultimately possess her. But I feared I would end up hurting her. If the wolf blood of my father, a wild Midnight Lupus who had mated my mother, took control of my body, my man-beast cock would be more than she could handle.

But my intentions were not driven by lust. I had connected to her, hearing Flame's pleas in my mind as she struggled against the Captain's unwelcome molestation.

*I need to choke him, kill this monster!*

As I watched her struggle, anger overtook me. A primal urge to extinguish the source of her torment coursed through me. My uniform tightened around my chest and loins. Canine teeth lengthened in my mouth until I licked my lips and brushed back the snowy white hair covering my face.

I pounced from the table where I had been sitting, knocked over two men in front of me, and leapt toward the front of the pub.

*Hold on, Flame. I'm here!*

If I could hear her thoughts, maybe she might hear mine.

With a few powerful leaps, I rushed towards the Captain and knocked him off Flame. She tumbled to the floor. Our eyes locked together.

*I won't hurt you.*

She held her mouth, staring at me. In that fleeting moment, seeing her sprawled on her stomach with the top of her breasts spilling out of her damp blouse, I knew I would never be complete unless I mated her, filled her up with my man-beast cock, and marked her as mine.

Her eyes flickered. There was a look of terror on her face.

*What are you?*

Her trembling voice echoed in my mind. I hated that she feared me.

Before I could reply, the Captain punched me in the gut, and I howled in pain. But the raging Midnight Lupus deep inside me, the wolf blood of my father, had been aroused. I growled and threw myself on top of the Captain.

He tried to push me away. I grabbed and held him tightly, letting my sharp fangs pierce the soft meat of his left thigh through the fabric of his trews. I tasted blood as he screamed in agony. Soldiers rushed towards us, swords raised.

"Kill the beast!" the Captain screamed as I twisted my head back and forth, my fangs embedded in his leg.

I could see swords held above my head. The soldiers hesitated, unable to strike me without lancing the Captain's leg. He tried to push me away.

"Get off me!"

I let him go and scrambled to my feet, snarling at the soldiers who circled me with their swords, ready to strike me down.

Captain Hawke managed to get up with the help of his two officers. "Bring me the wench!" he screamed, holding his leg where I'd bitten into him. Blood oozed from between his fingers. A soldier threw him a rag, which he quickly tied around his wound.

The officers scooped up Flame and held her in front of the Captain. Still holding his bandaged leg with one hand, he reached under the poor girl's skirt with his other hand and cupped her between the legs.

"Leave her alone!" I snarled.

The Captain shot me a look of hate as he fondled Flame. "She belongs to me now. I'll take whatever I want."

"You monster!" I screamed, and as I was about to rush toward him, a thick arm gripped my neck tightly. A sword raised up over my head.

"Kill him!" the Captain shouted.

A sudden burst of terror filled me with a power I'd never experienced. I pushed away the arm around my neck and jumped out of the way of the sword.

I was badly outnumbered. Two men still held Flame as the Captain pressed his hand tightly between her legs.

I shot a glance at her.

*I will kill him for what he's doing to you.*

She stared at me with a look of confusion. I nodded before jumping at the men holding Flame and knocking them over, pushing her and the Captain over as well.

Soldiers rushed toward me, daggers drawn. One reached for an axe, and all the other soldiers in the pub were on their feet. Captain Hawke rose to his feet.

"Butch him!" He screamed. Though I was powerful, I could not fight off more than a dozen armed men. I would be no use to Flame if they got their dirks and swords into me. I had to escape and come back for her.

With a powerful leap, I jumped over the soldiers standing in front of the wooden door of the pub. I rushed it, hoping I had enough strength to knock it down. I rammed the door with every ounce of power I could harness, jarring it loose from the hinges.

With one more powerful lunge, I knocked it over and fell onto the frozen cobblestones. A fang pierced my lower lip as I hit the ground. My mouth filled with blood. I got up quickly and looked through the gaping opening into the pub, catching sight of Flame still being held by two soldiers.

I spoke the words to myself, hoping she would hear them the same way I heard her voice in my head.

*I will come back for you.*

And then, as soldiers began to rush toward me, I sprang down the snowy lane and disappeared into the thick forests of the Dunfeld countryside.

## 3

FLAME

Was it all a dream, a fantasy playing out in my mind? Who was the man in the corner of the pub talking to me as if he was standing right beside me but not making a sound anyone else could hear?

Was he even a man? He looked more like a wolf, his face covered in white fur, his eyes glowing red, and two fangs protruding from his mouth. And yet he talked to me and tried to save me.

But why? Who was he?

*What* was he?

"Take her to my tent!" the Captain shouted as I remained in his bony clutches, staring out at the open door at the man, or 'beast' who had knocked it over. "And fetch my surgeon!"

Captain Hawke removed his hand from between my legs where he had been trying to probe the folds of my womanhood. He yelled out in pain, holding both hands to the spot where the creature had bitten him so ferociously.

An image of the savage attack filled my mind. Yet the strong voice that had come to me was filled with caring concern.

*I will come back for you.*

The words echoed in my mind.

I smoothed my skirt as Captain Hawke found a chair and held his wounded leg, groaning in pain. If I could only harness my Fae powers, I might be able to save myself from this monster. But try as I might, any magic in me, the daughter of a Fae mother and a human father, lay beyond my ability to harness it.

The only magic I could manage was communicating without speaking to the man-beast creature.

"Fetch her dry clothes," Hawke ordered one of his officers. "And bring her grandfather to the camp."

"Leave him alone," I pleaded. "He will pay you what he can."

"Shut your mouth, wench!" Captain Hawke grimaced, holding his thigh as he yelled at me. He was obviously in great pain and taking his anger out on me. "I will deal with him as I see fit. Now leave until I decide what to do with you."

**A**fter I was given dry clothes and ordered to wash, I was led to Captain Hawke's tent. Two armed soldiers stood guard outside, their intent obvious by the way they gaped at me. should be used to it by now.

Though I tried to dress modestly and keep my appearance as plain as possible, men in Dunfeld always seemed dumbstruck around me. I cursed my pouty lips and green eyes, my breasts, which had filled in so large and full that they now strained every outfit I wore.

I did my best to hide my chest from view, along with my wide hips and narrow waist.

And as the Captain had inquired, I was indeed ginger all over. The entrance to my womanhood was covered with soft, apricot-colored hair.

Waiting in the tent, with the soldiers guarding outside, I pondered what would happen when Captain Hawke arrived. He had tried to kiss me, fondle me, and get his fingers into the opening of my pussy. I was a virgin and inexperienced in the ways of men, though I felt the heat of passion listening to the stories of Prince Aiden and his bride, Elva.

Gossip about Aiden's chivalry, not to mention his horse-like cock, which now belonged exclusively to his wife Elva, was all my girlfriends whispered about when we found ourselves alone. I blushed at the lewd details of the stories but felt a warm wetness between my legs, imagining what it would be like to be intimate with such a man as the dark and dashing Prince Aiden.

By early evening, I had drifted off to sleep on the narrow bunk in the Captain's tent. I woke suddenly to the brutish barking voice of Captain Hawke.

"Get up!"

I rubbed my eyes and slowly managed to raise myself up.

The Captain had removed his red jerkin. The jacket, embroidered with gaudy gold silk tassels, hung on a pole in the corner of the tent. He approached me, massaging his crotch as he eyed me up and down. I was disgusted by him but unsure how I could escape from this horrible excuse of a man.

I tried to focus on choking him again, hoping to harness the Fae powers I knew beat deep within me. It was a wasted effort, although he did grimace ever so slightly and hold his neck a moment before he stopped a few feet in front of me.

"Undress," he ordered. "Slowly, so I can see every part of you."

I hesitated, trying to summon any magic I might possess to use against this vile monster. He flinched but kept rubbing the bulge in his trousers.

"I said undress," he repeated darkly, "or your grandfather will pay for your insubordination."

An image flashed in my mind—my grandfather's head being pressed to the floor under the boot of a soldier. I began to unbutton my blouse. When I undid the final button, I let my top hang open, glaring at the Captain.

"Let me see those big fucking tits," he groaned, rubbing his cock through his trousers.

Did I have a choice but to expose myself? I opened my blouse for him, revealing my naked breasts. He reached for one, squeezing and kneading the large globe before pinching the small brown nipple.

The Captain moaned. "The King will be pleased to have you as his third-wife. A virgin, no doubt?"

I scowled at him without replying.

"You know, I could try you myself and hand you over as a fuck doll. But you're worth much more as a pure maiden, unspoiled for King Shane to open for the first time. A virgin third-wife is a rare prize, indeed. Your cherry will be my gift to the King. Soon after, he will reward me as general of the entire Braeyork Royal Command and King's Guard."

Standing almost naked and exposed to the Captain like this deeply shamed me. I glanced at the opening of the tent. Could I dash for it, run, and get past those guards? Would I freeze, running half-naked into the cold twilight of a freezing winter night?

Before I could do anything, one of the guards rushed into the tent. As he approached the Captain, I tried to cover my naked breasts.

"Sir, Omar, *her* grandfather," the guard said, pointing at me, "has agreed to give you his entire harvest, one hundred and ten bushels of wheat, if you release his granddaughter. And he will pledge to acquire two gold coins."

The Captain laughed, pushing my arms aside, resuming his fondling of my breasts with one hand. "Excellent! The King will be pleased." With his other hand, he gripped my chin, looking into my eyes.

"But I wonder what is worth more? All of your grandfather's harvest? Or your virgin cunt?" He snorted. "Maybe... both?"

Without looking away, he barked an order to the guard. "Tell him we accept his offer. Arrange to pick up the wheat in two days." He lowered his head and added darkly. "And after you do, make sure Omar will never talk about how we took his harvest *and* his granddaughter!"

The burly guard chuckled, glancing at me. "He won't say much when I cut out his tongue!"

"No!" I cried, pushing away the Captain and taking a step back. I stood tall, straight, with my naked chest exposed to both men. "Do what you want with me, but please, *please*... I beg you. Do not hurt my grandfather!"

The Captain smiled. "You drive a hard bargain, ginger. But I accept. If you do exactly as I instruct you, your grandfather will not be mutilated. Do you understand? And afterwards, I will have your ass, leaving the rest of you pure and unopened for the King." He slobbered. "You understand, wench?"

"Yes," I cried, tears filling my eyes.

"Take off your skirt and show us your ginger pussy."

Trembling, I pushed down my skirt, letting it fall around my legs. My shame was tempered only by the hope of saving my grandfather. I tried to cover myself with my hands, but the Captain grabbed my wrist and swatted them away.

19

He stood close, equal to my height.

"Now, you will perform for me," Hawke commanded. "For both of us. Touch your pussy and play with your tits."

The guard smiled and began to squirm. I glanced back and forth between the two men. I wasn't sure if I could really go through with such a despicable request.

"Do it!" the Captain barked. He turned to the guard. "Johnson, remove your trousers. Show her how big she makes your cock."

Johnson laughed. "Yes, sir. Been hard rubbing myself, dreaming about fuckin' her all day."

"No, Johnson. Her cunt belongs to the King. But she can please you in other ways."

Fear gripped me as I watched the burly guard lower his trousers and unbutton his shirt. He pulled out his erect cock as he eyed me with a look of pure debauchery. He stroked his organ slowly up and down, the purple-tinged head popping out from the foreskin covering it.

"Touch yourself, or I will fuck you with my fingers," the Captain grunted.

I knew there was no escape. I squeezed one of my breasts, staring at the guard slowly stroking his cock. His mouth hung open as he stared at me.

"That's it, wench," the Captain urged as he lowered his trousers and exposed his own organ. His cock was smaller than the guard's but just as hard. "Touch your clit, ginger.

Get that cunt nice and wet. I want to see the look on your face when you cum."

The rudeness of his command and the wanton nature of his request disgusted me. But I had little choice but to comply. I touched my tiny bud, my 'clit' as he called it. My girlfriends laughed at how they would let Prince Aiden kiss and tongue their 'clits' all day long. That image always took me over the edge – the Prince tonguing my little bud with his big, wet tongue.

I closed my eyes and continued to massage my breasts, brushing the smooth palms over my erect nipples. As I did, traced the outline of my pussy lips before bringing my long middle finger up to my clit, slowly circling it.

I had done this a few times alone in the privacy of my bed-chamber but never imagined touching myself before two grunting men stroking their hard cocks.

Deep rage filled my thoughts. But also, and with deep shame, I felt how wet I was getting standing here exposed like this, touching myself while these two men stroked their cocks.

Yes, I was being humiliated, but my open pussy lips and erect clit betrayed me.

"That's it, you little whore. You'll make such a good third-wife for the King. After he fucks your virgin cunt and uses your asshole a few times, he will share you with his friends," the Captain growled. "You'll take a cock in your mouth, another in your cunt and, of course, one in your ass. All at the same time. Would you like that, ginger?"

His hoarse voice grew husky and dark. I feared the situation would soon get out of control.

I opened my eyes for a second and watched Johnson stroking his cock as he stared at me, touching myself. I had never seen a man stroking his cock. The guard moaned as if in a trance. I fought to quiet my own moans.

"Now, Ginger. Would you like to taste it?" Captain Hawke's words shocked me.

"No!" I cried. I could never do such a thing. But I had dreamed about tasting the cock of Prince Aiden. taking it in my mouth as my friends all claimed they would also gladly do. Perhaps such an image might serve me now to survive this perverse act that I was being forced to perform.

"On your knees, now!" the Captain commanded. "And keep touching your clit until you make him cum in your fuck-hole mouth."

The foul words stung me, but before I could react, the Captain's hand on my bare shoulder forced me to my knees in front of Johnson. He shoved his hard cock toward my face. The engorged purple tip brushed my mouth.

"Lick the head, ginger. And play with your clit while you suck him. I want to hear you cum when Johnson shoots his load in your virgin mouth and then all over those big white tits."

I looked up at the Captain stroking his own cock. He was a sick man.

There was no hope now. I had to comply with this depraved request. I opened my mouth finally and began to lick the head of Johnson's cock, tasting the drops of cum already seeping from it. I gagged as his fingers wrapped around strands of my hair, tightening his hold at the back of my head as he pushed his engorged organ into my mouth.

I closed my eyes as he began to pump in and out, fucking my mouth while he held my head. His cock slid over my tongue to the back of my throat, and then he eased back a little, grunting and groaning.

What was I doing? I had only imagined that wolf creature promised to come back?

I prayed he would.

"That's it, Ginger," the Captain growled. "Take all of him like the true fuck doll you really are. Keep touching your clit. Make yourself cum when you get a mouthful of his fuck seed."

The biting words snapped me back to the horrible reality of what was being done to me. Fighting the urge to bite down on the cock in my mouth, a voice suddenly filled my mind.

*Stop! I'm here.*

# 4

THERON

A s I slowly approached the Captain's tent, outlined brightly under a starry winter sky, I sensed Flame was in danger. I could hear her voice in my head as I made my way closer, careful to stay hidden behind the dense pine trees surrounding the clearing.

*I have to help my grandfather.*

I did not understand how I could hear her inner thoughts.

*I need to do this wicked thing to save him.*

If she was alone in the Captain's tent, I dreaded to think what 'this wicked thing' Hawke was perpetrating upon her. The image of that loathsome man touching her at the inn played in my mind. I knew what evil the Captain was capable of, having witnessed his ruthless manner many times as he terrorized poor men and women across Braeyork.

Each time I watched in horror, my wolf blood raging inside me. More than once, I had fought to restrain myself from letting it consume me completely. Each time, I wanted to take revenge on the Captain for laying waste to so many lives in the name of collecting taxes and tithes.

Yet, I did nothing to stop him.

But seeing Flame at the inn today was more than I could bear. Now, it was personal. She was not only the most desirable maiden I'd ever encountered but also strong and determined. And perhaps, like me, someone who kept a secret hidden deep inside her.

I crept closer to the opening of the tent. Only one guard stood outside. I overpowered him, felling him with a quick fist to his gut. He lay gasping and fled into the woods before I could tie him up.

Laying on the ground, I brushed snow off me and heard Flame's voice again in my mind.

*I can't do this.*

I had to act quickly. At the entrance to the tent, I peeked through the flaps and held my mouth in shock at the sight of Flame naked, on her knees, eyes closed. One of Hawke's men used her mouth like she was a fuck doll.

And Hawke stood there, urging her on. Was there no limit to this man's depravity?

"That's it, Ginger," Hawke grunted. "Play with your clit. I want to hear you moan when Johnson shoots his load in your mouth, and I spurt all over your big tits."

Anger overwhelmed me as I glanced around to see if they held swords.

No. Their weapons lay on the ground.

The two men were consumed in their lust. My face tightened as my fangs grew long, and I tensed for the kill. Wolf blood flowed through me as my glowing red eyes narrowed. The sight of Flame's innocent mouth being violated enraged me.

*Stop! I'm here!*

I screamed in my mind before yelling aloud for all to hear, "Stop!"

Flame pulled her head back, and the guard's cock popped out of her mouth. He turned toward me.

Captain Hawke froze, still holding his own erect organ. I pounced on the guard, no doubt confused by the sudden change from having his cock sucked to fighting for his life.

The advantage was mine. I bit into his arm as I punched his soft underbelly. I followed it with a series of sharp blows, still biting the fleshy meat of his forearm.

He yelled and pounded me with his fists. I landed another blow to his gut and let go. He fell over, winded, writhing in pain.

The Captain rushed over and grabbed his sword even though his pants were still down, with his flaccid cock drooping between his legs. I could just make out Flame cowering off to the side.

"Now you die, beast!" Hawke screamed, gripping the hilt of his long sword with both hands. He waved it in the air, shrieking before swinging it around and slashing at me. I dodged the sword, but he quickly brought it around the other way and lanced me. The tip of the razor-sharp weapon pierced my fur-covered cheek.

It took a second for the pain to register. The taste of my own blood infuriated me even more. I rushed toward Hawke, but he swung the sword again, slashing my shoulder.

I flinched with the new pain searing through me and pounced on him, knocking Hawke over. I gripped his neck as the dazed guard slowly rose to his feet.

*Look out!*

I heard Flame's voice scream in my mind as the wobbly guard reached for Hawke's fallen sword.

*Grab it!* I yelled back in my head.

She dashed over and lifted up the sword. She stood naked, waving the weapon at the guard. The soldier held his arm where I had managed to get my fangs into his flesh.

"Grab her!" Hawke gurgled with my hands still holding his throat. I squeezed him tighter, on the verge of extinguishing this pathetic man from the world forever.

Flame waved the sword like some mythical creature—a naked, redheaded warrior goddess. Though there was a fire in her eyes, I guessed she was no trained fighter. Her chances against a battle-hardened soldier, even a wounded one with no trousers, were dim at best.

The soldier gripped the end of the sword. She tried to pull away, but he snatched it from her. She screamed, then closed her eyes and clenched her fists. Her mouth contorted tightly, and suddenly, the guard dropped the sword and clutched his head.

I watched as Flame kept her eyes closed tightly while reaching her arms out, clenching her fists as if she were strangling the guard.

"She's a witch!" The guard yelled, slowly backing away. "She's trying to kill me!"

I relaxed my grip on Hawke's neck. I didn't believe Flame was a witch, but she had managed to harness some kind of magic. I couldn't blame her, but the Kings' Guard would hunt her down mercilessly if this man died.

*Stop! Don't kill him.*

She opened her eyes, caught mine for a fleeting second, and then collapsed on the floor. I leapt to my feet, grabbed the fallen sword in one hand, and, in the other, scooped up Flame's limp, naked body.

With the sound of Captain Hawke and the guard moaning and gasping for air as they lay on the floor of the tent, their trousers still down around their legs, I raced out into the winter night, carrying Flame in my arms. I threw the sword into the woods, wrapped her as best I could in my tunic and bolted into the dark forest.

I headed for the abandoned shelter I'd found earlier today. The deep gashes from Hawke's sword tore at me like spikes that had been driven through my body.

But I had no choice but to keep running.

## 5

## FLAME

F rigid winter air stung my nostrils. My nearly frozen bare feet and ears screamed in pain. I was being carried somewhere by someone…

*Are you okay?*

The voice in my head must have come from the creature carrying me. Was he an animal or a man?

*A man. I'm Theron.*

How could he read my thoughts? And how could I hear his words? He kept moving steadily ahead as I tried to blink my eyes open.

Through the darkness, I could make out the outline of towering trees. Moonlight reflected softly from freshly fallen snow on the ground as we made our way forward through the dense woods. I was almost naked, except for some garment loosely wrapped around my shoulders, barely covering my chest and stomach.

My bare legs dangled down under the firm arm of the man-creature carrying me. My naked ass pressed into the crook of his elbow.

"Stop!" I finally shouted. "Let me go!"

We stopped, but he did not loosen his grip.

I looked up at the man-creature holding me. I was sure his face had been covered in fur when he burst into the tent. But now, all I could see was a few days' growth of beard and a deep gash on his left cheek. Blood oozed from the cut.

Our eyes locked together. He was breathing hard from the exertion of running, his chest rising and falling. I squirmed up and down, still locked in his embrace.

"You're hurt," I said. "Put me down. Please."

He hesitated. "You have no boots."

"I don't care!" I cried.

He nodded, then slowly lowered me to the snow-covered floor of the forest, blanketed by the bright white moon. The icy ground stung my feet.

"Thank you for helping me," I said, dancing on the snow, wondering how I would manage half-naked with no boots. "But I'm okay now. I have to get back to my grandfather."

"Let me help."

What did he want, this half-man, half-wolf creature? Theron? And how could he read my thoughts? I kept prancing in the snow, pulling the tunic around me against the cold night air.

Ouch! Ouch! My feet were freezing. I didn't need his help—just his footwear.

"Wait!" he chuckled. "I'll give you my boots."

Theron crouched down and started to untie the laces of his heavy boots. I crouched down, aware the tunic wrapped around me was open and that the rest of my body was exposed to his gaze.

As he began to undo his laces, I stared up at him. "Who are you? What are you?"

"I'm Theron," he replied, "My father was a Midnight Lupus and my mother…" His face contorted in pain. He grabbed his shoulder. "Oh damn!"

"What is it?"

"The sword lanced my shoulder."

He grimaced, clenching his teeth and holding his eyes shut. Blood dripped from his cheek, and a drop fell as a crimson splotch on the white snow. I touched his cheek, trying to wipe away the blood. He flinched, but I kept my hand on his face.

"You're hurt," I said quietly. "Your face is cut bad, and I think your arm was slashed pretty deep."

"I'll help you find your grandfather," Theron gasped. "But first, let me take you to the shelter I found. You need warm clothes, and I need to clean my wounds."

The shelter was further away than I anticipated. Despite his injuries, Theron carried me in his arms, trudging on and on through the woods.

"I found an old hunting lodge," he mumbled, carrying me up and down the forest hills. "It's covered in moss and dirt, but it's dry, and there's a stove. It's warm."

I had so many questions running through my head. Was his mother human?

*Yes. She was human.*

His voice was in my head again, reading my mind and answering without speaking.

*Are you a Fae?*

His query startled me. I had never told anyone that my mother was born to Faerie parents and my father to a Fae mother. Only my dad's father, my grandfather Omar, was human.

"We're both half-things," he said out loud, slowing down as the path between the pine trees narrowed. A steep incline lay ahead. "The King beheads creatures such as us. I've watched it far too many times."

Half-things.

I'd heard the term before, always spoken with fear and disgust. And everyone in Dunfeld knew there was a bounty of three gold coins for turning in a half-thing—plus a place of honor at the beheading.

He was right. I was a half-thing—the same as him.

"Yes, I have Fae blood," I finally replied, although I guessed he already knew. I had never spoken these words to anyone before, afraid even to admit the truth of who I was to myself. "But I never knew what I could do... until today."

"When I lose control of my emotions," Theron panted as he strode, "and I'm overcome with rage or passion, my wolf blood takes control."

He was breathing heavily now. We slowed as the hill got increasingly steep. His legs sunk into the deep snow, almost up to his waist, touching my naked backside with icy kisses. Each step became a struggle. Theron started gasping.

"Put me down!" I finally cried.

Theron wobbled, still holding me. Up ahead, near the top of the ridge, I could see the contours of a dark roofline. It was no more than fifteen feet in front of us.

"Put me down!" I repeated.

There was no response. Theron kept moving forward. "We're almost there," he whispered, "just another few..."

He shuddered, and we began to keel over. We landed atop a deep snowdrift, my face planted into a blanket of fresh snow. I sputtered a moment, the shock of the cold against my bare bottom and legs spurring me to rise.

I wiped snow from my eyes. Around Theron's shoulder and head, the blanket of white snow grew dark with a deep crimson tint. His wounds must be deeper than I thought.

"Theron!" I screamed.

There was no response. I had to get him up to the lodge somehow. I glanced around. "Theron!" I yelled again.

He lay completely still with an expanding halo of blood red snow crowning him. He had to be faint from losing so much blood. With great effort, I managed to get my arms under his shoulders and drag him a few inches. He was a dead weight. There was no way I could get him all the way up the hill.

Closing my eyes, I focussed all my thoughts. I tapped into a strength deep within me and managed to pull him all the way up the hill before I collapsed beside his stiff body at the entrance to the lodge.

I wasn't sure how long we both lay at the entrance to the little snow-covered wooden lodge. Whatever Fae strength I had managed to harness was exhausted.

Sweat covered my face from the effort of dragging Theron up the hill. My bare chest glistened with moisture and beads of sweat. I wrapped the tunic around me and, with one last grunting effort, pulled Theron inside the lodge and shut the door behind us.

Glancing around, I saw the glowing seams of a coal stove in the corner. It kept the room warm and provided enough light for me to see. There was also a stone hearth on one wall and a bed of straw covered with blankets on the other. In the middle, two stools stood near a weathered wooden table. What was left of a thick wax candle sat atop it, cold, dirty and dead on a rusty pewter dish.

Leaving Theron lying on the floor, I lit a piece of straw from the burning coals inside the stove and used it to light the candle wick. An old scuttle held a few lumps of coal. I threw it all into the belly of the black iron stove.

The fire in the hearth had burned down to a few glowing embers, but with pieces of dry firewood nearby, I quickly coaxed it back to life, blowing hard until I was rewarded with a burst of bright orange flame. I piled on more wood, and it began to burn quickly.

There was now ample light for me to examine Theron's wounds. I crouched down beside him on the floor and touched his cheek. The blood on his face had congealed around the gash. He would carry the scar on his left side for life.

But it was his shoulder that most worried me. The white shirt sleeve of his right arm was drenched in blood. I had to get his shirt off and clean the wound. I began to unbutton his shirt when he opened his eyes.

"What happened?" He glanced around the room before looking back at me. "How did you…"

I leaned in closer, self-conscious that I was naked from the waist down. My breasts glimmered with a glaze of perspiration. I stopped unbuttoning his shirt, suddenly feeling very exposed to someone I barely knew. Except for Theron's tunic, which I wore and had not buttoned back up, I was naked.

He had saved me from the deplorable Captain Hawke and the equally disgusting guard. What would have happened if Theron had not come along when he did? I would have tasted the guard's cum seed in my mouth, and no doubt the Captain would have violated my asshole.

"Why did you come and help me?" I asked, wondering if I had left one horrible predicament only to find myself in an even more dangerous one.

Theron closed his eyes and drew a deep breath. I needed to remove his shirt and look at the wound, but could I really trust him? I knew he was injured, but here we were, alone and miles from anyone in Dunfeld village.

And I was more or less naked and about to take off his shirt.

*I won't hurt you, Flame.*

I sighed. He could hear me thinking. Could I read his mind the way he did mine?

I closed my eyes. Within a few moments, I began to feel deep, excruciating, throbbing pain. My right shoulder was suddenly on fire.

I was feeling *his* pain.

"Owwww…" I yelped as a hot knife pierced my flesh.

"Flame," he moaned. "Release yourself."

I stood up and shook my head. I had to clear my thoughts, think of something else, anything except him. I remembered my grandfather grooming his horse and tilling the fields. Picking berries, tending sheep…

Finally, the ache began to relax its hold upon me.

If that pain was what Theron was experiencing, I needed to help him in any way I could. I wasn't sure how he wasn't screaming in agony, but somehow, he found to absorb the pain. His long hair hung over his forehead, pointing backward. Although sweat formed on his forehead from the pain, he did not complain.

I crouched down again and sat on my knees. "We need to get your shirt off and clean your wound. I've patched horses after a fall, and I can stop your bleeding with any luck. And then wrap the cut."

"Thank you," he moaned and closed his eyes.

*I'm a lucky man.*

I smiled at his words filling my head. I had no idea how we could communicate without speaking, but at the moment, I didn't care.

"You won't be so lucky if I don't find something to clean that wound," I replied.

I worked quickly to unbutton his shirt. I pulled it open and gasped at seeing his smooth, hard stomach and the rippling muscles of his broad chest. I was expecting he would be covered in thick hair, but only a light layer of black hair was visible.

I had never before seen a man with a body such as his, so incredibly fit, hard, and well-defined. I stared at his nipples, centred on each side of his heaving chest. He looked as strong as an ox but as sculptured as a racehorse.

I blushed at my reaction to seeing him bare-chested. He was gravely wounded, and I was ogling him like a foolish schoolgirl.

*You're not foolish, Flame.*

Damn! I had to try to hide my private thoughts from him, or this could get embarrassing. "Stop it," I scolded gently. "Or I'll read your thoughts too."

He grinned at me, opening his eyes a moment before clenching his teeth and scrunching his eyes. I had experienced his pain. Now, I needed to help him.

Scooting over, I gently cupped my hand behind his neck. "Can you sit up so I can get the rest of your shirt off?"

Theron slowly pulled his muscular torso upward, with me helping him up into a sitting position. I pulled his left arm out of his shirt and then, ever so carefully, coaxed his wounded right arm from the bloodied sleeve.

Tossing the shirt aside, I moved over and examined his injured arm. There was a deep, open gash. I knew from working with horses that if it was not cleaned and dressed right away, it would fester and rot. It could be his slow, agonizing journey to the grave.

"I'll look for some salt and spirits to clean the cut. And then I'll use your shirt to wrap it. Okay?"

I waited a moment for him to respond. His body shook, trying to answer me.

"Thank you, Flame," he whispered. "I'm in your debt."

## 6

## THERON

H er soft hands on the back of my neck provided such welcome, warm comfort. Flame gently massaged my skin for a few moments before she stood up and padded away.

My shoulder throbbed as if gripped by a sharp-toothed beast. I needed to think of something that might help me endure this torture. I glanced at Flame, wearing only my red tunic jacket, which she had buttoned up. Despite the agony racking my body, the sight of her lifted my spirits.

Her beauty was beyond any I had ever seen before. And how I could read her thoughts so plainly was a mystery. I had been with many women but had never experienced anything like this. It was as if the thoughts in her head also lived within mine.

"I found something," she called out from the corner. "Salt, and I think, a flask of Black Brandy. I can make a healing paste with this and soot from the fire."

"Good," I whispered.

The torment wracking my shoulder was getting worse. How much more could I take? I closed my eyes and prayed to the gods to help me through this ordeal. And I thanked them for Flame, without whom I would surely give up and wither away.

"This is going to sting," she whispered, crouching close to me. "Bite as hard as you can."

I opened my eyes. She held a stick of wood in her hand. I opened my mouth, and she placed it between my jaws.

"Ready?" Flame asked.

I nodded, the stick clenched tightly in my teeth. She reached for a handful of the paste she'd made and pressed it into my open cut.

*Fuuuccccck!*

I bit down hard on the wood as pain ripped through me.

"I know it hurts, but it'll purify the wound and keep away disease," Flame said. I nodded again, blinking my watery eyes.

She worked quickly, washing away the paste with Black Brandy before applying another stinging salve. When she was done, she washed the cut with melted snow and wrapped it tightly with some of the material she had ripped from my shirt. She also cleaned the cut on my face the same way but kept it open to the air, explaining it would speed up the healing process.

Finally, she pulled me up to my feet. I stood close to her, my head a foot higher than hers. I already felt a little better.

She reached for my hands and held them as she looked up at me. "You need to rest now. And I need to leave."

I stared down at her. "Are you sure?"

Flame sighed, looking away. I could hear the voices in her head struggling. She wanted to run, find her grandfather and get away from me. But she also wanted to know me. She was drawn to me but afraid. She fought her desire, fearing what I might do to her.

I had to stop reading her thoughts. It was wrong. I shook my head, wishing not to hear anymore. But her voice kept filling my mind.

*I can't have these feelings. It's wrong how he makes me feel– as if I was an experienced woman of the world and not an innocent virgin.*

Her words stirred me in a way I had never felt. I wanted to hold her and protect her, keep her safe from harm, and never let anyone do her wrong. But my wolf blood pounded through my loins, filling me with a beastly lust to mount her, fuck her deeply, and claim her as mine.

My cock swelled in my pants. I tried to push away such impure desire, beat down my wolf instinct to mate my bitch here and now, whether she wanted to be taken or not.

I prayed she could not read my thoughts, cursing the part of my animal brain that consumed me when I had such impure thoughts.

"Flame, you are free to go. I won't try and hold you back." I gripped her hands, trying not to stare at the deep cleavage between her white breasts squeezed into my crimson tunic.

"Yes," she replied. "That's what I should do."

She spoke the words but made no effort to leave. Although I tried not to, I could feel her tangled emotions. She wanted to run away, to flee from me and help her grandfather.

"Thank you, Theron, for rescuing me. I don't know what I would have happened if you had not come..." she hesitated," but I really need to go."

Flame stared at me as I fell into her eyes. The distance between us heated as her thoughts betrayed her words. She wanted to know not only who I was, but 'what' I was.

And to know, unlikely as it may be, if there could be something more between us.

*Forever.*

I heard the word in my head.

But I could not tell if the thought was mine or hers.

# 7

## FLAME

How could it be?

How could I stand here, so close to this... this man... half wolf, who I hardly knew and feel such longing?

I should find some trousers and boots and run away, far away. I should run and help my grandfather.

And yet, all I really wanted was to be in his arms. And to be loved and, dare I say it... to be his completely, to let him make me a woman tonight and lose myself in his strength. I wanted to know what he felt like to be taken by him, to be his.

And only his.

We shared thoughts and spoke without speaking. I could even experience his pain as if it were my own. I knew it was wrong, but I felt so deeply connected to him that I wanted him to have me in the way I knew he desired.

The way I desired as well.

"Flame," Theron said quietly, "I won't stop you, please know that. But it's late, and you'll not make it far without proper clothes and boots. Stay and rest until morning, and then I will help you find your grandfather."

He hesitated, his dark eyes peering down at me, penetrating in their dark intensity. "If that is what you want, Flame."

I nodded, suddenly overcome with memories of the terror in the Captain's tent – a hard cock shoved in my mouth., another one threatening to spurt all over me and then violate my asshole. I was so grateful that Theron had come when he did for me.

My eyes watered, and my heart pounded out a reply to my head.

"Yes," I whispered.

He drew me into his arms and pulled me closer. I turned my head, laying it on his massive chest. I sensed something changing within me, listening to the pounding of Theron's heart through his bare skin.

We held each other like this, not talking out loud but having a conversation nonetheless.

*I will keep you safe, Flame.*

I smiled, my head pressed to his chest, listening to the rhythm of his heart.

*And I want to do the same for you, Theron.*

My feelings for him were not something I had ever experienced. But I was afraid of losing myself to him or to anyone. All that had ever brought was pain.

He released me and walked to the other side of the lodge. He sat down upon the bed of straw covered in furs.

The light from the stove and the hearth had grown dim. The candle had burned down, and I shivered. It was getting colder with our only sources of heat nearly extinguished.

"Come and lie here with me," Theron said from the corner. "There are enough furs to keep us both warm."

Hesitating momentarily, I watched as he held up one of the thick fur stoles. He was right, and though I was afraid of what might happen if we lay together, him bare-chested and me wearing only his tunic, I trusted him.

He arranged the furs on the bed, stood up, removed his boots, and lay back down on the bed. "Come, Flame. I'll keep you warm," he motioned, studying my face, "and safe."

I shivered again from the wintry chill taking hold of the lodge. Warm comfort beckoned. I crawled on top of the bed, and Theron covered me with a blanket of furs.

We turned to each other. I felt safe with him but wanted to be held, his bare chest against my skin. I unbuttoned my tunic, opened it, and moved closer. He welcomed me until our faces touched and our bodies pressed together tightly.

"Flame, I am trying not to, but I hear your thoughts."

I tensed at his words. Did he know my desire for him? How much had I revealed?

"Don't worry," he whispered. "I feel the same. I want to know you more than I ever wanted to know anyone."

I pushed closer against his bare chest, pressing my breasts against his skin. He reached his good arm around me and softly rubbed my back, and then his hand wandered up higher to the back of my neck. I closed my eyes with the comfort of his gentle, strong hands. He kneaded my neck and the back of my head slowly and carefully.

I melted under his touch.

"You know they will come for me," he whispered. "And when they do, you must run and leave this place. I will do whatever it takes to keep you safe, but these men will stop at nothing and…"

His words trailed off. I reached an arm around him and felt the strength of his thick neck. Our faces were so close, our lips barely an inch apart. I could almost taste his words as he spoke, but now he has closed his eyes, pain written across his face. What was he thinking?

Closing my eyes as we lay pressed against each other, I searched his thoughts.

*I will die if they harm her. No matter what the cost, I will slaughter them all if they so much as touch her again. I don't care what they do to me as long she is safe.*

His fingers stopped massaging my head, and I sensed a darkness in his thoughts and a fury growing within him.

"Theron," I whispered as tears welled up behind my eyes. "Thank you. But…"

I wasn't sure how to thank someone willing to give his life to save mine.

He opened his eyes, and I could see they were as moist as mine. "Flame," he breathed in a deep voice, "don't worry about me. I will do what I must to protect you."

We stared at each other as the echo of his words drifted away. An orange glow from the dying fire reflected in his glistening eyes. What little space remained between us was far too much. I pulled his head closer to mine, needing to feel his lips upon mine.

He didn't resist. Our mouths pressed together with a warm tenderness that was hopeful, excited, and yet somehow shy and hesitant. We revelled in the thrill of our lips touching, an explosion of joy cascading through me like nothing I had ever experienced.

I needed to kiss him deeply, to know his mouth, to feel the strength I knew lay deep within him.

*Just as I need it, too.*

His voice was in my head, and I didn't care if he could read my thoughts. I wanted to… needed to… would do anything to… be his.

Our mouths opened to each other. His tongue explored me, taking control as I felt his body stiffen. We kissed for a long time, back and forth, thrusting and pulling apart, only to return to soft and gentle kisses.

With our lips still pressed together, I whispered, "I want to be with you."

"As do I, but it might never be. You don't know those men the way I do." His moist breath excited me, even as his words warned me to keep my distance.

No matter what might happen when the sun rose, tonight I needed to be his. I wanted to lie in his arms and be one being with him. I knew it was wrong, but we might never have this moment again.

I leaned back, sat up, and removed my tunic. Now I was completely naked, and except for his trousers, there was nothing separating our bodies from knowing each other intimately. I hovered over him, the outline of his face staring up at me. There was a hunger in his eyes and a glow that was no longer a reflection of the dying fire.

His dark eyes gleamed shades of crimson. I closed my eyes and could still see the red glow pulsing in his. In my mind, I could feel his desire for me and the conflict ravaging him.

I laid back down and pressed my body against Theron.

I needed all of him in the deepest part of me.

## 8

## THERON

How could I deny her what she most needed? Though I did not want to read her lurid thoughts, they filled my mind with the intensity of her needs.

*Take me, Theron, all of me. Fill me with your love so we can be one.*

Flame did not know what would happen if I let my arousal fully take control. Already my eyes were clouded in a blood-red wash, and my cock straining against its tight prison. My wolf side threatened to consume me with a dangerous lust that I needed to subdue.

But the beast in me longed to ravage her perfect body, mate her here and now with all the force built up inside my loins. Her full, soft breasts pushed against my chest, my heart pounding blood to every inch of me.

I had to stop now before it was too late.

*No Theron. Don't hold back. Mate me now.*

"Flame," I whispered in reply. "My wolf side is something I must control. If it takes over, I could hurt you."

She put a finger to my lips. "Theron. You saved me tonight. You are willing to die for me. I am in your head just as you are in mine. Could anything hurt two half-things sharing one mind? Two half-things that could finally be made whole?"

Flame lowered her head. "We might both die before the sun sets again. I need to feel your love inside of me, at least once, to know you, to be mated with you, in case we are torn apart forever."

I cradled my hand around her neck. My cock throbbed with need, wanting so badly to be freed from my trousers. I had to mate Flame and mark her as mine. I needed to fuck her, push deep into her virgin pussy until my seed was released into her fertile cunt.

And yet, a tiny part of me screamed to preserve her innocence.

She pulled my head to her, and we kissed again deeply with urgent longing. Her thoughts filled my mind as if she were whispering in my ear.

*I want your seed inside me. This might be our only chance, and I want to know your love before it's too late, before you're taken from me.*

Her words extinguished the last vestiges of hesitation. Fur thickened on my face, and my arms and legs bulged. My cock screamed to mate her.

As we kissed, I moved a leg between hers and rubbed against her moist pussy. She ground into me, and I began to dry hump like we were fucking. She moaned with each thrust, my leaking cock searching for her wet entrance, frustrated with the thin cloth of material separating our bodies from joining together as one.

Still, a voice deep, deep inside screamed for me to stop.

"No!" she cried as I paused my thrusting between her legs. I pulled my lips from hers and searched her eyes.

"I'm no better than those men in the tent," I whispered. "I want you more than I have ever wanted anyone."

I trembled as she reached and touched the soft fur covering my face as I spoke. "I don't want you just for tonight, Flame."

She lowered her head. A tear trickled down her cheek. She began to sob. She was my angel. I had to hold her, comfort her, taste the salt of her tears.

"Theron," she sobbed, "don't ever leave me. *Ever.*"

The wolf blood coursing through my veins slowed. The man part of me spoke instead. "I won't, Flame... so long as I draw breath into this body."

We held each other, and I let her cry, her tears falling upon my lips. I don't know how it could be, but wrapped together like this, hearing each others' thoughts and the feelings buried inside us brought me a joy I had ever known.

*I won't ever leave you either, Theron.*

We kissed with the excitement of knowing our deepest desires were the same.

As we lay in each other's arms, we began to let our hands explore. I reached for the round orb of one of her full breasts, squeezing it in my hand and circling the taut nipple with my finger.

She did the same to me, stroking my chest and pinching my nipples. Our kissing grew more passionate as we touched each other. I felt her hand wander lower down my hard stomach. She stopped just above my trousers but kept rubbing and teasing, trying to get her fingers inside my pants as I cupped her breast.

My cock twitched as she undid my belt.

"Let me touch it," she whispered.

The fur thickened around my face. I needed release. I let go of her breast and pushed my trousers down around my legs, freeing my stiff cock at last.

Her mouth covered mine as her hand wrapped around the head of my cock. I moaned as I thrust my tongue into her mouth and returned my hand to her breast, pinching her nipple.

As I massaged her perfect tit, she worked her hand over the swollen head of my cock. It was already leaking cum. She stroked the head slowly, working her fingers all the way around it, sliding over the veiny animal knots. I gasped with the pleasure she was bringing me.

"This is mine," she whispered, lowering her hand around the shaft of my throbbing cock. "It belongs to me. Only to me. No one else."

"Yessssss," I moaned. "Only to you."

I kneaded her tits, going between them both, feeling the cum rising in my cock, as it grew larger in girth until she could barely get her hand wrapped around it.

"Oh my," Flame whispered. "You were right."

I groaned as she stroked all the way down the shaft of my swollen member and then slowly came back up and covered the wet head, smearing drops of cum over it.

A deep guttural sound formed in my throat as her pace quickened and my balls engorged. I was so full of cum, I needed to release. My grunts became urgent.

"Cum for me, Theron. Cum for your mate… your bitch. Shoot your seed all over me."

Her words burned through me. I let out a blood-curdling shriek as her soft hand fucked me until I finally could not hold back another moment.

A thick, heavy load of cum spurted from my cock, all the way up to Flame's stomach. I shot load after load, screaming in pleasure as she milked every drop, then slowed and released her grip around me.

I lay trembling. She raised her hand to her mouth, my hot seed dripping from her fingers. She tasted it as one final tiny spurt shot from my pulsing wolf cock.

We sat in silence for a moment. I tried to catch my breath. Flame cooed as she licked her fingers. I knew, staring at her in her naked perfection, tasting my warm cum on her fingers, I would forever belong to her.

*And I forever to you, Theron.*

Her voice filled my mind as I lifted myself up. I needed to hold her and never let her go.

But before I could do so, a disturbing sound came to me from far off in the distance. I closed my eyes to try and concentrate. It was the deep-throated baying of bloodhounds on the hunt, searching for their prey.

And they were very close to finding it.

# 9

## FLAME

I didn't hear the sound right away, but from the look on Theron's face, I knew something was terribly wrong.

"Bloodhounds!" he gasped. "They're close!"

I recoiled in fear. The baying of excited bloodhounds was the sound of death. Whatever creature being tracked would soon be hunted and slaughtered.

"They must have followed us here and…" Theron hesitated.

I lay naked before him with the taste of his warm cum still lingering upon my lips and sticky fingers. I had grown almost as excited as he had with the pleasure I had given him. I felt his excitement both in my hand as I stroked the full length of his thick knotted shaft and massive cock head, but also in my mind.

I heard his lurid thoughts and experienced the over-whelming power of his passion. I felt it in my aching, empty pussy with each stroke.

And then, when I felt his cock begin to throb, a wave of pleasure swept my mind as if I, too, were about to explode. With each spurt, I felt his release deep inside me, stronger than any time I had ever touched myself.

"Flame!" Theron cried. "They're getting close. Listen to me very carefully." He pulled up his trousers and stuffed his still-hard cock into them. He sat down on the bed and held my cheek.

"You must get away. Run to safety. I don't care what they do to me, but I would sooner die than let them touch you again."

I shook my head. "No, we'll fight them together. We are both half-things. I am not afraid."

At this reply, his tone changed. Anger seemed to fill his eyes, a red glow returning to them.

"No, Flame!" he growled with an intensity that frightened me. "I know what they will do to you. You are not ready to fight them."

"I am!" I retorted. "I feel something, a power I can use against them, and then, we can both…"

Theron rose and lifted me with him, cutting off my pleas. I was naked, and he was bare-chested as he took hold of my wrists and leaned in closer. "Losing you would be worse than any axe, blade, knife, or whip they can use against me. You must run. Cover yourself in these furs and leave. Now!"

"No!" I screamed. "Not without you!"

"I said go," he growled.

He was changing before my eyes. His eyes glowed, his face was again masked in white fur, and fangs protruded from his lower lip. "Leave me to do what I must do," he slobbered.

Theron turned around and headed for the door. I stared a moment, gasping for a response. Without turning, he repeated his orders in a dark voice as he walked out the door.

"Run away. Forget about me."

Once outside, I ran, clutching the furs. Although it was still dark, the light of the moon on the white blanket of snow helped light my path. I didn't stop running until I reached the top of a bluff overlooking the hunting lodge.

I hid beneath a wide, bushy pine tree, standing on a bed of dead, brown needles. My feet were wrapped in fur stoles, and I wore the thick hide of a brown bear around my shoulders. I crouched under the tree, pushing the branches away slightly to view what was happening below.

The baying of the bloodhounds grew louder. Theron stood near the front door of the lodge, completely covered in white fur. He held an axe in one hand as he glanced around. His eyes looked up to where I hid beneath the tree and then quickly looked away.

"Forget about me." His voice echoed in my head.

Was that what he wanted? I was confused by his cold tone and his words.

*Forget?*

I wanted to be his in every way. Desire still quivered inside me, an aching need to live and die with him.

Could he read my thoughts from a distance?

*Theron, I am close and safe. Come with me. Save yourself before it's too late.*

I poked my head through the pine boughs to see if he might react somehow. If he had heard me, there was no indication by his manner. I closed my eyes, hoping I might hear his voice in my head.

*I told you to leave.*

How could I just up and run with the sound of bloodhounds growing louder and the angry shouting of soldiers? The light of their torches revealed their movement through the woods. And even more alarming, they were headed up the bluff toward me.

Theron snapped his head back toward me. I pushed out past the pine boughs until he could clearly see me.

*Run, now! And don't come back!*

Theron pointed up past the bluff, north, away from the village and the camp of the King's Guard. The torches were approaching quickly, the dogs baying in a frenzy, howling and barking with the scent of their prey so close at hand.

And they were headed straight toward the tree where I hid.

"Hey you! Stupid fucks!"

Theron yelled and screamed at the soldiers. He ran towards them, his axe held high above his head. All the dogs and soldiers stopped running up the bluff and turned around to face Theron. He howled and cursed as he plowed through the deep snow like a rabid animal.

"Get him!" one of the soldiers cried.

Another soldier, this one trying to hold back three lunging bloodhounds, turned to Theron, who paused a moment, allowing them to get closer. He stood waiting and then, at the last moment, fled down the hill with soldiers and dogs following close behind.

More soldiers appeared through the trees. All of them gave chase toward Theron, fleeing away down to lower ground.

He had saved me once again.

But I doubted this time he would be able to save himself.

## 10

## THERON

How could I have been so careless? I knew the ways of Captain Mason Hawke and this butchering regiment of the King's Guard he commanded. And yet, I had done nothing to cover my tracks or disguise my scent. It had been easy for the bloodhounds to find me.

And to find her.

A group of soldiers had me trapped, pushing closer to the rock wall behind me. I could take a few of them with my axe, but there was no way to escape from all the men threatening me, pressing closer with their swords raised.

"He's a half-thing!" one of the soldiers, a Marshall I recognized as Harper, a ruthless killer of unarmed men and women, yelled out, wielding his sword above his head. "Theron's a fucking wolf! A man-beast!"

I snarled, holding my battle axe high in the air. Besides Harper, there were other heavily armed soldiers and a few younger men who had recently joined our company. They all hesitated, knowing they could overpower me, but not without losing a limb and getting maimed in the process.

My only concern was to ensure Flame had gotten away from this band of raping murderers, particularly Captain Hawke, who would violate her and, if he ever found out she was a half-thing, use her body in every possible way before beheading her.

*Flame.*

Why had we bonded so quickly? Why had I fallen so hard and fast and let her do the same? Being with me meant she would be hunted, found, used, and executed. I had to find a way to hide my feelings for her and make her think I despised her. If she read my thoughts again and knew how my heart was hopelessly devoted to her, she might do something foolish.

I would gladly die here and now rather than let Flame suffer the indignity Mason Hawke and the King's ruthless guards would bring upon her.

*I am a beast, Flame. I can't be yours. Find someone worthy of you – a man, not a monster like me.*

I had to fill my mind with thoughts to drive her as far away from this horrible place as possible.

"Attack!" Harper cried.

Three soldiers to his left and three to his right came running at me. I waved my axe back and forth, menacing anyone who dared get within a few feet. I knew some of these men. I had fought with them and also knew most had been forced to fight for the King. But they had become well-paid soldiers, numb to the horrors of battle, intoxicated by the spoils of pillaging villages, torturing men, and violating women.

I struck the first soldier, Bannon, who drove toward me with his sword drawn. I knocked it away from him, taking his hand off cleanly with my axe. He fell to the ground, screaming in agony. But in that brief moment, two other soldiers jumped me, and then Harper barrelled through and kicked me hard in the groin.

Buckling over in pain, I howled before trying to bite and punch the soldiers wrestling me to the ground. It was too much, and someone got a noose around my neck. It was quickly tightened until I was choking. They began to pull, throwing the end of the rope over a thick branch to hang me.

"No!" Harper cried. "He belongs to the Captain."

I stood before Captain Mason Hawke in his tent an hour later, bound with heavy ropes, stripped of my boots and trousers. My head hung low, bruises covered my body, and I ached so deep I wasn't sure how I even managed to remain standing.

The light of the new day was breaking. Despite my physical pain, my heart felt lighter. Flame had escaped and, with any luck, had fled far away. If she had gotten my message, perhaps she would forget her foolish maiden desires. I had saved her in this same tent yesterday, and perhaps she had been overcome with a sense of duty to nurse me.

Her affection, her beauty, and her innocence were something I would treasure and carry to my death. I would leave this world with a smile on my lips at the memory of her perfect face and smile, the fragrance of her skin, and the taste of her tears. No matter what they did to me, they could not take away the joy Flame had given me in our one and only night together.

"A fierce man-beast?" Captain Hawke snorted. "A wild half-thing?"

He laughed, shaking his head back and forth, holding a bowl of steaming mulled wine in his hand. He surveyed me, tied and helpless. "You're pathetic. I'll be sure to salute your severed man-beast head after we drive it onto a wooden stake."

Hawke sipped his drink with a smirk. "But I'll tell you what. We won't castrate if you tell me what you did with my Ginger." He stepped closer and squeezed my lips. I tried to spit at him, but he only pressed my mouth together tighter, and all I could manage was a weak dribble.

"Where is she?" he screamed, releasing my lips.

"Fuck you."

I could see anger flashing in his eyes. Nothing he could do would hurt me as long as Flame was safe.

"Fine," Hawke snarled. "Have it your way."

He spat on my face, turned, and walked away. A few minutes later, two soldiers led me away. In front of a roaring bonfire to fight the winter morning chill, an axeman and a soldier with a long black dagger stood holding tankards of dark frothing ale.

"Stand up!" the one with the dagger yelled. "I get to take your manhood!"

The axeman snorted. "And I, yer head." They both laughed as they slurped their drink. I had seen them do this before. The hatred inside me, not so much for these two men as for the Captain and King Shane who ordered and relished such atrocities, burned inside me. My hatred was my strength.

I would use it to endure what awaited me.

When they were done drinking, farting, and belching, the soldier with the dagger approached me. "Going to enjoy this, half-thing!" He nodded, smiling. "Unless you want to tell the Captain where his Ginger pussy is hiding? Then ye can go straight to the axe."

I met his eyes. "Fuck you."

The soldier laughed. "Something ye won't ever do again!"

He reached for his dagger and lowered it to my groin. I closed my eyes and saw Flame running to safety in my mind.

*Run, my love... as far away as you can.*

I opened my eyes and tried not to show fear. The black eyes of the soldier held mine, and I knew the moment was at hand. He lowered the dagger, smiling without taking his eyes from mine. I girded myself for the bite of his knife.

"Stop!" A stern voice called out.

I turned toward the voice. It was a tall man in a flowing robe atop a white steed. Everyone stared, then knelt down as King Shane dismounted from his horse and made his way toward me.

~

"Is it true what I was told?" the King asked as he approached me. The soldiers remained on their knees, cowering at their sovereign. "You are a man-beast? Half wolf and half man?"

I looked away without answering.

Bound in chains, standing naked in the dirty snow, I must not have appeared to be much of anything, much less a fierce beast. Still, as powerless as I was, I preferred not to engage with the King who now sat upon Braeyork's throne after the death of his father, King Rolfe.

The new King had beheaded his own stepmother, young Queen Ursula, within days of his father's death. He claimed she was an adulterer and a fornicating witch. The axeman mercifully took the Queen's neck cleanly and swiftly. But I knew, as did many in the King's Guard, that Ursula carried a child in her womb when she was executed. Her body was burned within the hour.

King Shane had prevented an heir to the throne from drawing a single breath. Stories of the gruesome beheading and the burning of the headless corpse had recently begun to spread across Braeyork.

65

The King grew impatient with my silence. "Answer me if you wish to live!"

Captain Hawke stepped forward. "Sire, I have seen it myself. And my men, too. When he is aroused, his wolf blood takes charge of his body. As you have commanded since the day you ascended to the throne, we behead unholy half-creatures such as this. He tried to trick us, joining as a soldier in your Guard, until he revealed his true nature to us yesterday."

"Aroused?" the King repeated, still eyeing me. "Aroused in anger?" He looked away a moment and then stroked his chin. "What about... in lust?"

No one replied.

King Shane stepped closer to me, talking as if I was not standing directly before him. "If we let him live, a man-beast could be a powerful member of my Guard. Everyone knows I despise all manner of half-things," he said, lowering his voice, "but such a beast, under my command, serving in my Guard? That could be useful—a powerful weapon to inspire fear and respect of the Crown."

The King turned to Captain Hawke. "Bring this man-beast... does he have a name?"

"Theron," Hawke replied tersely.

"Bring him to my lodging in Dunfeld."

An hour later, I was escorted to where the King made his residence in the village. It was the only stone house for miles, the home of a prosperous landowner. I was fed beef and bread and given trousers and a tunic to wear.

My feet were shackled with metal clamps and chains to ensure I would not flee. Inside the stone house compound, I was locked in a cavernous stable of some sort, with bales of hay and tools all around, a stone floor, and slats of light shining through from open port holes high overhead. A bed of straw lay at the far end. I was dead tired, and though I wanted to plan some sort of escape, I needed rest.

Sleep took hold of me the moment I dropped onto the straw bed.

## 11

## FLAME

Where could I run to and be safe? How could I save my grandfather? And how could I just flee and leave Theron behind?

I remained hidden under the pine trees for a long time after I watched them capture Theron and lead him away. I tried vainly to read his mind and to talk without words as we had done last night. But there was nothing.

Only silence and an empty feeling of failure gnawing inside me.

What had happened between us? How could I have become his and he mine in only a few hours together? Was such a thing possible?

Maybe it was the rush of feelings after such a frightening and horrible ordeal. Or perhaps it was merely lust from the excitement of two strangers thrown together, finding themselves alone in life-and-death circumstances. I mused that it was nothing more than a scared woman comforted by a strong man.

No.

It was much more. We were both outcasts belonging neither to the world of Braeyork humans nor to the faeries of the forests or the hunting beasts of the plains.

And how we could hear each other's thoughts, apparently only when physically close to one another, was a thing quite beyond my understanding.

But still, I wanted Theron. I had never met anyone so physically powerful yet so loving and gentle. I had never known anyone willing to sacrifice everything for me, though we had just met. His gruff manner telling me to forget him was done to protect me by driving me away, far away to safety.

Of that, I was certain.

I began to make my way through the woods. I had no plan, but I would not let Theron die without trying everything I could to save him. And I was not willing to forsake my grandfather. Captain Hawke might be a merciless monster, but I would be cunning and ruthless as well, given half a chance to confront this evil, pathetic man.

I did not fear death if I could rescue the only two people I cared for in the world.

A sudden noise behind me broke into my thoughts—the snap of a branch. Or perhaps a twig? Was someone or *something* following me? I pulled the furs on my shoulders closer together and crouched low in the snow. All my senses were sharp as the first light of dawn began to trace the outline of bare tree branches in the woods.

*Snap.*

Again, a faint sound, but it rang sharply in my ears. I remained close to the ground, clutching my fur garments, searching for the source of the sound. And then I saw a winter hare, almost pure white with an outline of gray around its mouth. It sat perfectly still, turning its head in a stilted manner, searching for signs of danger.

As I watched the hare, I sensed a pair of eyes watching *me*. It was not the hare I had heard but something much bigger and more ominous. A mountain lion or a timber wolf prowled nearby.

I was being hunted.

Closing my eyes, I focussed on every sound and feeling. A sense of hunger flooded my mind. My nostrils flared, and I detected strong body odor. I heard the sound of shallow breathing; the prey was female, close at hand, an easy kill.

Primal thoughts filled my mind, but they were not mine. I was in the head of the animal hunting *me*.

Again the strong body odor. I realized it was coming from between my legs—my still damp pussy. It was giving me away to the beast tracking me. I had the smell of an aroused female from my encounter with Theron.

My eyes blinked open at the sound of a threatening growl. It was a wolf. I was certain—a Midnight Lupus probably, the same as Theron's own father. Its mind was filled with the urgent pangs of an empty stomach. I searched for the eyes of the animal, knowing it was close by in the woods or hidden behind a low-lying brush.

A twig cracked. The winter hare scurried into the woods, and the massive form of a full-grown wolf came barreling toward me.

I stood up, letting the furs covering me fly into the air, focussing my mind on the beast about to attack. I gripped my hands in a choking hold.

*Halt! Or I'll kill you!*

The hunting wolf slowed but kept advancing. I stood my ground, naked, covered only by my long red hair. It was now me against a massively powerful, pure white Midnight Lupus that could down me in a single leap.

*I will kill you if you come one step closer.*

The wolf stopped, its hollow eyes fixed on me. I was in its head now, smelling *my* fertile female scent. I was an easy kill.

I had slowed but not stopped it. I closed my eyes and focused all my strength on trying to inflict pain on my attacker. If not, I would die.

In my mind, I bit viscously into its neck. The taste of warm blood filled my mouth. A hollow whine rose from the wolf. It dropped to the ground. I did not wish to kill the animal, only frighten it.

*I warned you.*

If the wolf understood, I could not tell. It paused and growled, but I could still feel its rage. I needed to be sure it got the message. I closed my eyes and, in my mind, reached under his belly and yanked at the hanging testicles of the wolf.

The resulting howl was mixed with a whimpering cry, and with one final frightened look, my dazed attacker ran off into the depths of the snowy forest.

## 12

## THERON

Daylight had slipped away by the time I opened my eyes. I lay dazed, trying to unscramble my thoughts when the barn doors opened, and King Shane entered. Two young women followed behind, both fair-skinned and striking in appearance and dress.

A sheer bodice covered their breasts, and a flap of chainmail dangled between their legs. Another piece of it hung over their bare bottoms. The skin of their long, shaved legs was visible on either side of their chainmail skirt. I presumed they were naked beneath their dangling coverings.

Two guards followed and stood at the open door, cross-bows drawn.

The King pulled up a wooden stool and sat down near the foot of the straw bed. The two women stood on either side of him, smiling curiously at me.

"Theron," King Shane spoke as he sat on the chair. "I've come to offer you a chance to live, provided you are a man-beast as my officers claim. If you serve me, I will ensure you are handsomely rewarded."

I said nothing. Could I use the King's preoccupation with me to my advantage?

"These are two fuck dolls I brought with me," the King said, turning first to the dark-haired woman to his right. "Sasha, who is now twenty-five." And then, touching the leg of the blonde woman to his left, "and of course, Misty, who just turned twenty-one."

Both women were finely manicured and groomed.

The King raised his hand under Misty's sheet of chainmail covering her womanhood. "She is always wet for me and screams like a wild animal when she cums. Just your type, I suspect."

He fondled her under the chain skirt until her knees buckled. She released a little gasp. "Her pussy is soaking wet."

I stared at the scene before me. I knew what the King was trying to do—arouse my wolf blood, and though I tried to fight against it, my cock twitched at the lewd display and the passion in Misty's moans as the King fingered her.

He kept his hand between her legs for a moment until he finally pointed toward me. "Sasha, Misty, on your knees. Go to him."

Sasha smiled at me and fell to her knees. Misty whimpered at the release of the King's hand from between her legs, then dropped to her knees as well. They began to crawl towards me slowly, cat-like in their movements, licking their lips as they sized me up, crawling closer on their long, bare legs.

I glanced at the King and then at the two guards by the open door, both clutching cross-bows. I wouldn't get far with shackles around my legs, but still, I weighed my options. The women on their knees continued approaching, never taking their eyes off mine. Misty kept her mouth open, tracing the outline of her lips with her tongue.

When they were directly in front of me, they halted. Each took hold of one of my legs, massaging my calf, purring and whimpering as their soft hands reached around, circling my knees in wide motions. I stared down at them. The touch of their fingers, the sight of their firm breasts through their sheer blouses, and the cooing noises they made stirred desire deep within me.

I wanted to resist, thinking of Flame, even though I hoped I had driven her away for good.

"You can have them both," the King smiled. "In any manner you like, all their fuck holes are yours to fill." He clapped his hands. "Ladies, undress each other."

Sasha and Misty stopped touching me and turned to one another. They stood up, took each other's hands, and smiled knowingly. I couldn't help but stare at these two beautiful young women as Sasha reached around and removed Misty's sheer top, exposing her perky, milky white breasts, each centered with a small dark nipple. Sasha fondled Misty's breasts, pinching her nipples and licking them before giving each a playful bite.

I clenched my legs together, my cock straining inside my trousers.

Now, Misty turned to Sasha and removed her blouse. Sasha's tits were bigger and heavier but looked just as firm. Misty sucked each breast until Sasha moaned and then pushed her away.

"Kiss her," the King commanded in a stern voice. "Taste her."

The two bare-chested women began to kiss passionately. I was shocked at the sight of something I had never imagined before. And try as I might, I could not fight my excitement. As they continued to kiss, their hands wandered down their narrow waists and under each other's chainmail flap.

"You see, Theron?" the King said, rising from his chair. "They are trained fuck dolls. Their tight cunts are already wet at the thought of your animal cock stretching them open."

Sasha and Misty kept kissing as they fondled each other's pussy. From the way they moved and the sounds they made, it was obvious they were finger fucking. I tried to look away, but the King commanded me otherwise.

"Watch as they taste each other."

Both women removed their hands from between the other's legs. Sasha offered her middle finger to Misty, who sucked it greedily. Misty did the same to Sasha.

"Misty, give Theron a taste of your pussy."

She removed her finger from Sasha's mouth and stepped closer to me, seated on the bed. Misty's lavender fragrance filled my nostrils. Her bare breasts and erect nipples were almost in my face. She slipped a hand between her legs and moaned as she touched herself lewdly and bent down until her face was close to mine.

She purred and touched her wet finger to my mouth. She rubbed the bottom of my lip and pushed it across my tongue. "You like the taste of me?"

I closed my eyes. I hated myself, but fuck yes – I liked the taste of Misty. My cock was throbbing in my trousers. My wolf blood was taking control. As she teased my mouth with the taste of her pussy, I felt my heart racing as my fangs grew longer in my mouth.

Misty removed her finger from my lips and offered me one of her firm breasts. She shoved one tit in my mouth, and I suckled it, squirming now with the need to release my cock from its tight confines. I could feel my body changing.

"That's good, Theron. Suck her young tits," the King urged. "Sasha, offer him yours too."

Misty pushed her breast into my mouth one last time, then pulled back as Sasha offered me one of her even bigger tits. Her dark, wide nipple waited for my mouth. I pulled her to me and sucked on the fat tit as she crushed it into my face.

As I suckled her, Sasha reached down and laid a hand over the bulge in my trousers. I growled at her touch. Strands of white hair began to grow on my cheeks. She kept stroking the bulge through the material, her palm brushing back and forth,until I thought I was going to explode.

But I knew what was happening. I was being used, and I had to stop them. I pushed the women off of me and stood up.

"No!" I cried. "You can't control me like this!"

Misty and Sasha cowered at my feet, both topless and flushed, staring up at me. I wanted to mount and fuck both of them, but I was determined not to let the King take control of me as his man-beast soldier. I would not terrorize his subjects, no matter what he offered me.

"Look at you, Theron," the King barked. "Fur is growing on your face. And I know what you need—to mount and breed these fuck dolls. It is *who* you are. It is *what* you are. They are yours to use. Take them and show me if you are as powerful as my men claim."

I stood panting.

It was true.

I wanted to fill Misty and Sasha with my throbbing wolf cock, and release the cum building up inside me into their soaking wet cunts. But then, I would be no more than a circus animal made to perform. I had wolf blood, yes. But no one owned me.

A plan began to form in my head. "I will take both women and show you the power of the beast inside me. But only if you remove these shackles and let me fuck them properly."

King Shane smiled. "Theron, you're more clever than I gave you credit. Not just a beast, but a cunning man who thinks he can outsmart a King."

He stood up and approached me. "You will show me if you deserve to live and if I can trust you. All in good time. But first, I must see for my own eyes if your life is worth saving."

The King waved to two soldiers at the door. "I want this man's arm shackled and strong guards to hold him while he fucks."

Now I understood why the King held power. He took no risks.

My plan to use Misty and Sasha to transform me fully into a man-beast in order to kill the King or hold him hostage to ensure that Flame would be safe had backfired. Instead, my hands and feet were now shackled in heavy chains, guards with crossbows stood at the door, and four hulking men held me spread-eagled in front of King Shane and his two topless fuck dolls.

"Now," he commanded, taking his seat a few feet before me. "Let's see the animal that beats within your heart, the beast that lives within your trousers."

He pointed to Misty and Sasha. "Undress him, suck his cock, get him hard for your cunts."

I was helpless against the steel shackles and the guards holding me prone. Misty and Sasha approached me. Misty kissed my cheek softly as she unbuttoned my tunic, one copper button at a time. Her naked breasts rubbed against me as her fingers opened my tunic, slowly revealing my chest to Sasha, who had dropped to her knees to unbuckle my belt.

Anger at the King, sitting and smiling at the show he had ordered, combined with the lust enveloping my body at being undressed by these two beautiful women, seized every ounce of me. Misty had my tunic completely opened and began to caress my chest, squeezing and pinching my nipples.

"Oh my," she whispered into my ear, "you are so strong, so firm. You're making me even wetter."

I wanted to ignore her, but my body was reacting to her touch and words, to her sweet fragrance and her naked tits, which she pressed against my bare chest. Her lips found mine, and she pushed her tongue into my mouth.

Sasha had unbuckled my belt completely and began to lower my trousers down around my legs. My angry cock, swollen and hard, was finally free.

"Oh look, Misty!" Sasha cried.

Misty removed her lips from mine and dropped to her knees beside Sasha. I couldn't help but stare down at these two bare-chested women kneeling on either side of me, my stiff cock twitching and growing even larger between their two open mouths.

I panted, feeling my fangs poking out through my mouth as Sasha gripped the shaft of my cock, struggling to get her hand around its full girth. I was almost naked, with my trousers around my legs and my tunic hanging around my arms. Four guards held me tightly prone. And now, as lust and anger combined within me, I was completely covered in white fur.

"Taste that fat wolf cock, Misty," the King barked from his chair. "See if you can get all of it in your mouth."

I struggled against the shackles even though I wanted so much to feel Misty's mouth take the head of my throbbing cock. The cum was already leaking out as I watched her lick off the first few drops and tease the underside of my engorged shaft with her wet tongue.

A voice inside me felt shame, but my wolf blood was stronger than my guilt. The voice went quiet.

Sasha watched, eyes wide as Misty opened her mouth and tried to get her lips around the head of my pulsing organ. "That's it, Misty. Just take a little bit," Sasha urged as she held my cock in place to feed it into Misty's waiting mouth, guiding her head toward me.

The shackles around my ankles and wrists held me firmly in place, with men holding the chains on either side of me. I boiled with rage at the King for yielding such dominance over these women and me. Yet I was also consumed with animal desire at the wanton sight of the fuck dolls so eager to suck me.

Misty managed to take almost the whole shiny head into her mouth. I felt an urge to pump, to push into her throat, but I could only thrust my hips so far. Two guards to my left, and another two to my right, kept me bound like a dog on a short lead. I struggled against the chains, but the guards kept me tightly restrained.

The animal within me craved more of Misty's mouth, wanting so badly to hold her blonde head in place and fuck her throat. My cock was taking control, and the last vestiges of the man inside me vanished. I howled and grunted at my bitch, struggling to take more of me between her wet lips.

It was too much. She gagged, slobbering and choking with the enormous girth and length of it. "Let me try," Sasha moaned as my cock slipped from Misty's mouth, shiny wet with her spittle.

Dark-haired Sasha had an easier time. I bucked my hips, and she managed to take almost half the length down her throat until she, too, gagged.

"It's too big," she cried as Misty crept closer. They both touched my cock, dripping with their spit. They stroked the knotted shaft up and down, looking at me, eager for my climax. I felt my knees weaken at their slow and rhythmic stroking. Cum was rising, and if they kept this up, I would shoot all over their faces.

"Stop!" King Shane yelled. "Remove your skirts, get on your hands and knees and show him how wet your cunts are for him."

Misty gasped. "No, sire. He's too big. He'll hurt us!"

The King rose from his chair. "I said take off your skirt and get ready for his cock. Or, I'll give you to the soldiers here."

The four hulking men restraining me hooted and leered at Misty. "We'll take turns with all yer holes," one of them yelled, "fill both of ye until you scream like stuffed pigs."

I yanked against the restraining chain held by the bearded man who had just spoken with such a hateful tongue. The chain came loose from his hand. I tried to do the same with the towering man on my other side, but soldiers brandishing crossbows rushed forward. I backed down.

"You are indeed a man-beast, Theron," the King smiled. "But I want a show." He turned to the guards. "Fasten the chains holding his arms to the iron rings on the wall behind him. Secure him well."

Guards dragged me backward. They fastened the chains around my arms and legs to the black iron rings on the stone wall, the same rings used to tether livestock.

"Now, Theron, I want to see both of my fuck dolls take your cock. Don't hold back. If I like what I see, I'll give you both of them—to breed or use as you see fit."

The threats to the two women had snapped my human senses back. Although I was still enraged with lust and anger, I did not want to hurt Misty and Sasha. "Let them go, and I will serve you, Sire."

I bowed my head in the best display of deference I could manage, though the wheels were turning in my head of how I might kill the King.

King Shane snorted. "You will fuck them as I command, Theron. If you refuse, I will hand them to my soldiers to use right now, and then I will behead them. I have new fuck dolls waiting for me to train at Braeyork Castle."

"No!" Misty screamed. "Sire, we worship you. We love you!"

Sasha gasped as well but was more reserved in her pleas. "Sire, you have taught us to serve all your filthy needs. We will go even further if you desire, but please, our bodies, all our fuck holes belong to you, for your pleasure, we will even take –"

"Enough!" the King interrupted. "I want to witness you both being fucked by this monster, this man-beast, to see if he deserves to serve within my guard. If not, I grow tired of this game."

The King began to rise from the stool.

"I'll fuck them," I shouted. "If you will give them to me after as you offered."

"Of course, Theron," King Shane replied, sitting back down on the stool. "I need you well taken care of for the new role I am planning for you."

Misty and Sasha, still topless, moved closer, and I prayed I could get my cock into their pussies without causing them too much pain. All the women I had ever fucked had struggled to take all of me.

With my arms and legs still shackled, my trousers bunched around my feet, my unbuttoned tunic hanging over my shoulders, and white wolf hair covering most of my body, I must have appeared a strange half-creature to these women. But they appeared grateful for my offer to save them, even if I could only do so by fucking them.

They draped themselves over me on either side, kissing my face softly and rubbing their hands over my broad chest. I wanted to whisper I would try to be gentle, but King Shane peered intently at us, and if I didn't play the role of a fierce man-beast, he might renege on his offer to spare the women.

I growled as they continued to kiss and caress me. It was done for the King's benefit, but Misty and Sasha had indeed aroused the beast within me. My cock stiffened as their hands wandered lower across my hard stomach. My knees buckled in anticipation of them taking hold of me. I may have had honorable intentions as a man, but if my wolf blood took full control, I might not be able to control myself.

"On your knees, ladies," the King commanded. "Offer your cunts like bitches in heat."

I howled.

Again, it was not just theatrics for the King. My wolf side needed to mount them, breed and claim them as the alpha male of the pack. A tiny human voice in my head urged me to be careful not to hurt these poor women. But I wasn't certain I could control the wolf.

Sasha stopped stroking me, got on her hands and knees, and wiggled her ass, still covered with a thin sheet of chain mail. I rubbed my legs against her ass, waving my swollen cock back and forth. I needed to get on my knees to fuck her, which was difficult with the chains binding my arms and legs. There was just enough slack to allow me to crouch down behind Sasha.

"Let me help," Misty offered. Kneeling beside me, she raised up the chain mail sheet covering Sasha's ass and caressed her two plump ass cheeks. Misty reached her hand between Sasha's legs. "Her pussy is soaking wet."

Sasha sighed and began to rock her protruding ass back and forth, grinding against Misty's probing touch. "Fuck me," she moaned.

I leaned in, and Misty took hold of my cock as best she could. She couldn't get her hand all the way around it but was able to guide it toward the swollen lips of Sasha's wet pussy hole. Misty rubbed the head of my cock back and forth over the lips, brushing Sasha's clit while trying to get her ready to take all of me.

Sasha moaned as if she was in a deep trance.

Thrusting my hips as Misty guided me, I felt the tight walls of Sasha's pussy opening up to my swollen ribbed cock. She was incredibly tight. I pulled back a little to let Misty rub the head of my cock around the outer lips of Sasha's pussy again. The King wanted a show of my ferocity. He needn't worry. The beast inside me was in control of my cock.

"Take it!" I growled. "All of me, in your fucking cunt!"

I glanced at the King, who smiled and squirmed on his stool.

"Oh, fuck," Sasha moaned as I thrust into her a little more, managing to push the head of my cock completely inside. "Owwww, oh, oh!" she cried.

"Misty, feed your pussy to Sasha!" the King barked from the stool.

"Yes, Sire."

Misty released her hand from my cock, removed the straps holding her chainmail skirt, and moved in front of Sasha. I almost exploded at the sight of Misty completely naked, her long blonde hair falling over her shoulders, squeezing her firm tits, while she ground her shaved pussy lips into Sasha's face.

My cock was shoved in about as far as I could get into Sasha. I tried pushing in a little deeper and withdrew until I was almost out of her pussy, before I thrust back in, slow and deep. She gasped even though she had taken only half of my cock.

I rocked back and forth slowly, sliding in and out, in and out. Sasha whimpered with each forward thrust. Misty cried out as Sasha licked her pussy hole and tongued her clit.

"Fuck her hard!" the King hissed.

My cock was wet with Sasha's cunt juice, but I could not completely penetrate her. Seeing her licking Misty's pussy, and the sound of Sasha's guttural moans as I pumped in and out of her from behind into the tightness of her pussy fed my animal desire. I had to fuck Sasha completely. The beast would settle for nothing less.

With one strong thrust, I pushed all the way inside as she screeched and raised her head from Misty's pussy lips. I felt the back of her womb momentarily, grunting and snarling with my conquest. Sasha's gasps turned to a whimpering cry.

A tiny voice inside my head urged me to stop. I glanced over at the King.

"Now use Misty," he commanded. "I want to see if she can take all that thing inside her tight little hole."

Misty glanced at me with a look of dread.

The wolf had claimed the first round, but the terror on Misty's face shamed me.

I nodded discreetly, hoping she would understand I would do my best not to hurt her. Still, the look of her shaved pussy, excited me. I pulled out of Sasha, my cock glistening from her wetness. She collapsed on the floor, moaning and whimpering.

But I was surprised that Sasha soon pushed herself up as Misty crawled forward and positioned her naked backside in front of me.

I wanted so badly to hold those perfect ass cheeks, but with my hands still bound, I had to wait while Misty crawled back a little further and pressed her pussy lips against my slicked cock head. I thrust my hips forward and motioned for Sasha to come closer.

She understood immediately and took hold of my cock, rubbing the head over Misty's pussy lips. "He has a monster cock," Sasha whispered to Misty. "Let him own you. Your cunt belongs to the beast."

Her words made my cock jump as Sasha rubbed the head around Misty's outer pussy lips. It slid easily over the soaking-wet entrance, but I needed to be inside of her. With Sasha guiding me, I pushed the head into Misty's wet fuck hole.

"Ohhhwwwooo!" Misty groaned.

"That's it, Theron, use her!" King Shane screamed.

I didn't need much encouragement. I wanted her pussy, which was even tighter than Sasha's. Misty moaned with noises I had never heard any woman make before as I rocked back and forth, each time pushing in a little deeper.

Incredibly, she took every inch of my thick, knotted cock. I was buried into her, pushing right up against the back wall of her pussy. I owned this female and every other bitch in the pack. My cock was what they craved, what they needed. I was full of seed and no longer cared to be a man.

I was a full-blooded Midnight Lupus wolf.

I felt the cum rising in my balls and heard Misty scream out, "I'm cumming!" I slowed and rocked back and forth, letting her ride out her pleasure on my cock.

She was perfect. But I could never be hers. I needed to mate for life.

But only if it could be with Flame.

The King wanted a show, and I knew how to give it to him.

"Sire, I will not mate them until I know they can swallow my seed. I want to see them take my cum all over their faces. And bow to their new master," I growled.

"Do it!" the King exclaimed. "All over them!"

Without hesitating, I pulled my cock out of Misty. "On your knees, bitches!" I commanded. "You heard the King!"

Quickly, Misty and Sasha got on their knees before me, their faces flushed, their breasts covered in sheens of sweat. I knew both their pussies were still wet from the fucking I'd given them. And now I would release my load all over their faces.

Sasha stroked my hard cock, still slick from Misty's pussy juice. As Sasha stroked, Misty leaned over and licked the head, then took it into her mouth. Sasha kept stroking, and I knew the moment of release was close.

"Make him cum!" the King yelled.

The head of my cock swelled even larger inside Misty's warm mouth. I trembled as my body prepared to shoot a huge load. Sasha popped my cock out of Misty's mouth.

"Fuccccccccck!" I shrieked, yanking the chains binding me as my body was wracked by a powerful explosion. I spurted thick, heavy ropes of hot cum all over Sasha's face as I yanked the chains with such fury I ripped them right off the wall.

I was still cumming, holding the chains high above me as Misty took my spurting cock back into her mouth. I shot another load before she gagged and choked. I pulled out of her mouth and aimed one last load of cum over both of their faces. They smeared it all over their big tits and then kissed each other, sharing the taste of my hot seed.

Completely exhausted, fighting for breath, and somewhat ashamed at what I'd done to these young women, I glanced at the King. He nodded at me.

"Theron, you are even more of a beast than I imagined. You've earned these two fuck dolls. I hereby gift them to you," the King announced.

"Thank you, Sire."

"But I don't yet trust you," the King added. "So, for now, you and your new bitches will remain locked up and guarded."

The King rose and began to walk away. "Take good care of them, man-beast!"

# 13

---

## FLAME

Wandering a long time through the dense forest, I had time to reflect on how I had managed to scare away the Midnight Lupus.

Somehow, I found a way to harness my Fae powers even if I didn't know how to control them or what I could do with such abilities. I kept heading toward my Grandfather Omar's cottage. I came upon it as daybreak began to lighten the eastern sky, slowing to weigh my options if I found him alone or if he had already been taken away.

I hadn't considered a third possibility, the one I stumbled onto—my grandfather tied to a chair, with two soldiers and Captain Mason Hawke interrogating him. I crouched low after spotting them through the little glass opening near the front door, which had been left open. I listened to the exchange happening inside.

"I told you no deal until you returned my granddaughter," Omar hissed.

"Your granddaughter was stolen by that half-thing who probably fucked her good before we managed to capture him," the Captain snarled back. "She's likely nothing more than a ruined whore if she rode that monster cock."

"Take that back!" my grandfather shouted. "Or nothing more will you get from me!"

I peeked my head around the open door, afraid of how Captain Hawke would respond to Omar's belligerence. The Captain pointed to one of the soldiers and motioned for him to step closer to where my grandfather sat tied to the chair. The soldier approached, drawing a long dagger from his belt.

"We'll take all your grain, old man, and all the gold you've hidden in the inn unless you tell us where that Ginger is hiding," Hawke sneered. "Or, if you don't feel like talking, we'll take your tongue too."

"I'd rather be a mute than waste another breath on scum like you!"

The other soldier in the cottage reached around Omar's head and yanked it back. Hawke took out his own dagger and held it up before my grandfather's face.

"Say your last words, old man!" Hawke barked as he gripped Omar's lower lip to try and force his mouth open. The other soldier began to choke Omar in an effort to get him to gag and open his jaw for Hawke's blade.

"Stop!" I shouted and ran into the cottage clad in hides and furry boots.

∼

I t took a few seconds for everyone in the cottage to recognize me, covered in fur stoles and a bearskin hide. I uncovered my face, revealing my red hair and pale white face.

"Flame!" my grandfather cried. "You're safe!"

"And a maiden still," I replied.

Captain Hawke held the dagger under his chin as he studied me. "The half-thing didn't mate you?"

"He saved me. Nothing more."

"So, you're still a virgin?" the Captain quipped with a sly smile.

I didn't wish to reply to such a crude inquiry, particularly when posed by a man like Mason Hawke. "Untie my grandfather, let him go and then you can take me as your prisoner."

The Captain approached me. I tensed up, wondering if I could harness my Fae abilities to keep him from touching me. I focussed my anger on Captain Hawke, imagining my teeth biting into the wound where Theron had already bitten him.

"On the contrary, Ginger, we'll keep him tied and gagged until we…"

The Captain stopped in his tracks.

"Fuck!" he groaned as he grabbed his thigh where Theron had sunk his teeth into him yesterday. He began to walk toward me, but I again conjured biting into his wound. "Shit, that hurts!"

"Untie my grandfather," I repeated. "Or your pain will get much worse."

"What?" Hawke looked confused. "What are you saying?"

"I'm a half-thing too, Captain."

The other soldiers standing near my grandfather glanced up with alarm. "Captain, be careful. If she's a Faerie, her magic could be deadly."

Mason Hawke stared at me. "She lying, trying to scare us into releasing her grandfather. We'll take her to the King, and he will see if her hymen is or is not intact. He already got a man-beast to bend the knee. I'm sure a virgin third-wife or a new fuck doll will please him even more."

King Shane had got Theron to bend the knee to him? Would we both end up serving a truly despicable King?

Saying anything more wasn't going to help me, Omar or Theron. I tried again to cause the Captain pain, but it seemed to have little effect on him this time.

Maybe Theron was right. I did not yet know how to harness my powers.

**A** few hours later, I followed the Captain on horseback. They wrapped me with a thick blanket and tied my hands behind my back.

I had been prepared in Dunfeld, forced to wear a new gown after I had been washed in a perfume bath. I was to be presented to King Shane, who had left this morning with Theron. I also learned, much to my dismay, that two young fuck dolls had been gifted to him by the King after Theron fucked both of them.

My grandfather rode behind, also tied and bound. Armed soldiers rode at the front and back of our little procession toward the King's camp some five miles down the road that eventually led all the way to the capital and Braeyork Castle.

Had Theron turned and pledged loyalty to King Shane in exchange for two concubines? Maybe Theron was more beast than man after all. How could I have let foolish romantic fantasies cloud my thinking?

All men were beasts inside.

Theron was also a beast on the outside.

I needed to find the key to unlocking my Fae powers. Perhaps Theron wasn't worth saving, but my grandfather needed my help, and I would not be the King's or anybody's wife—first, second or third.

And certainly not anyone's fuck doll.

## 14

### THERON

Although my legs were shackled in irons again, riding in the back of a covered wagon with Misty and Sasha for the past few hours made it bearable. The King was taking no chances. Armed soldiers on horseback rode behind us.

There were only three wagons in our little caravan: the one in which we travelled, the gold-trimmed wagon in which the King rode, and another covered wagon of cooks, servants and two members of his council. A pair of soldiers leading in front and another pair following behind provided our armed escort as we made our way down the long trail toward Braeyork Castle, where I was to be trained as the King's 'man-beast.'

I had no intention of serving him even though I did not know how or even if I could escape. But I would rather die than carry out orders for King Shane.

Misty and Sasha were a different sort of problem.

"Sir," Misty spoke quietly, sitting near my feet on a blanket on the floor. "I can never truly thank you enough for saving me, but I will try and please you. Often, sir, as much as you desire."

She wore simple clothing that did little to hide her pleasing shape, letting her robes fall open to my gaze whenever she moved. "Misty, that is not necessary," I replied.

Sasha moved closer. "Sir, you own us now. Without you, we would have…" she held her mouth a moment, "been treated very badly, I fear and then…" She grimaced, running a finger across her neck with a slicing gesture, "lost our heads."

I felt my own throat tighten. But it was for the shame I felt in allowing my wolf cock to penetrate so deeply and wantonly inside of Sasha. I had lost control. But that was no excuse.

"I'm sorry, Sasha, if I hurt you when I …"

I didn't want to speak the words. She caught my eye and nodded, her eyes moist.

"Thank you, Sir. No one has ever spoken words of apology to me before."

We all sat in silence for a moment. I wondered what kind of horrors they had endured in the service of the King.

Misty rubbed my pant leg. "And I'm sorry to admit this, Sir, but I love you for saving us. I know it's wrong, and I shouldn't have such feelings, but if you give me your seed, I will gladly carry your child."

Sasha shook her head. "Misty, you know fuck dolls are not allowed to be wives. We are not permitted to be bred and carry children. We must flush out our master's seed with the High Meister's poison rinse and–"

"Misty, Sasha," I interrupted. "I don't own you. No one should. If you want to have children with a husband, that is something you should do."

Misty pouted and rubbed my leg higher, up high between my thighs. I felt my cock twitch at her touch. "I belong to you, master. I will love you until the day I die and give you as many children as you want and always, always, take your cum seed… in any manner you desire."

"No, Misty," I replied gently. The feeling of her hand on my leg was difficult to resist, but I pushed it away. "My heart is spoken for already. And whether or not she and I can ever be one, I cannot be untrue to her."

"Master, no!" Misty cried. "Who is this woman? I will fight her, I cannot live without you!"

Sasha smiled. "You know nothing about love, Misty. Master has a wife, and we will serve him only as we've been trained to do, as his loyal fuck dolls."

"No!" I corrected. "I don't have a wife. And the only reason I saved you was to give you your freedom."

～

By the time the wagons stopped rolling a few hours later, Misty had dried her tears and grown quiet.

Sasha and I talked about how they could escape and where the two of them might run. The King had released them, but if anyone knew they were escaped fuck dolls, they would be cast out and permitted no society with anyone. They might even be stoned.

And they would never be allowed to marry.

The afternoon air grew colder, and we found blankets in the wagon for them to wrap themselves in against the winter chill.

"Tell the guards you need to relieve yourself, and then, once you're in the woods, run and do not look back," I explained. "I'll keep the guards occupied."

After Misty and Sasha were ready, they came and stood close to me.

"Thank you, master," Misty whimpered, her eyes moist with impending tears. "But my heart will always be empty without you."

She kissed my cheek, and I recalled the brief union of our loins. Someday, she would make her husband a *very* happy man, and hopefully, she would be able to raise a family of her own. She kissed me one more time lightly on the lips and stepped away.

Sasha took her place. "Thank you, good sir. I'm not as innocent as Misty, but I would have been honored to be yours. In any manner you desired."

"Thank you," I replied. "You are young and strong. Don't let anyone own you – ever again. I have faith in you, Sasha."

She kissed my cheek, and then, after a quick exchange with the guards who let them descend from the wagon to relieve themselves, the two women walked out of my life.

I sat a moment, praying they would make it to safety. I needed to help them by creating a distraction.

"Guard!" I cried out. "I need to see the King! I have urgent news!"

# 15

---

## FLAME

T he day's ride seemed to go on forever. My mind tried to sort through dozens of conflicting thoughts and feelings until I wanted to scream at the jumbled voices in my head.

I was everything.

And yet, I was nothing.

I was mostly Fae, but I could not control and harness my abilities. I was a half-thing and had found another half-thing who had swept me away with a thunderbolt of passion and, dare I say, *love*, only to forsake me and join the most wicked King in the history of the Braeyork Dominion.

The King who had beheaded his stepmother carrying a child in her womb—his own half-brother! A King who brought shame on the entire Dominion.

And Theron was willing to serve such wickedness?

I had wanted Theron more than I had ever desired anyone. I had glimpsed how two hearts might beat together, only to learn he had taken two fuck dolls for his pleasure.

My heart no longer cared to beat as one with his.

*Stop!*

I scolded myself for my endless loop of self-pity. The horses ahead slowed. In the distance, I could see covered wagons and smoke rising. It curled high, floating slowly in the still winter air, creating a lazy spiral before disappearing into the blue sky.

"Send a rider to tell the King we have arrived," Captain Hawke yelled at one of the soldiers, who nodded and gave his mount a sharp kick. I watched him ride ahead and talk to the soldier leading us, who immediately galloped toward the King's wagons.

In a few minutes, we approached the camp. As we drew near, I felt a strange sensation. A voice filled my head.

*Please keep them safe. I hope I have not sent them to their deaths.*

I had only ever heard the thoughts of one other person.

*Theron?*

If he was close, perhaps he might hear my thoughts too. But if he was now in league with the King, I needed to keep my thoughts hidden lest I reveal anything that might endanger my grandfather.

*Flame?*

I glanced towards the covered wagons.

Was Theron inside one of them?

My horse came to an abrupt stop. I glanced around and saw the Captain speaking with a tall figure, with a face I recognized from the painted portraits that hung in the public houses in Dunfeld. King Shane resembled his portrait but was rougher and fatter than he appeared on the canvas.

An icy feeling slithered down my spine as I watched him talking to the Captain, who pointed at me and then at my grandfather, bound on the horse behind me.

Two soldiers approached.

"Get down, wench," he ordered. "And be sure to bow to the King, or you'll get two lashes from me."

Wrapped in a wool blanket with my hands bound behind me, it wasn't easy to dismount, but I managed to get off the horse with some help. My grandfather was also assisted off his mount, and we both soon stood draped before the King.

I refused to bow to such a man and stood my ground defiantly.

"Sire, she's a natural ginger," Captain Hawke explained as if I wasn't standing there. "Ginger all over, full of spirit, and untamed. And, she's a pure maiden. The kind of virgin third-wife you've been seeking to break in and to train, Sire."

King Shane studied me, cloaked in a gray wool blanket. I glared at him.

"Let me have a look at what's underneath," he commanded with an air of privilege.

The soldier who had warned me to bow, ripped the blanket off me and tried to push my head down in deference to the King. I bucked my head and stood tall. The soldier slapped my face, landing a stinging blow to my cheek.

"Bow to your King, wench!"

I hissed at the soldier.

The King laughed and took a step closer. "She's a feisty one!" He touched my burning cheek where I had been cuffed. "What is your name, child?"

"Flame," I snorted, glowering at the soldier who slapped me. He looked familiar, and I now recognized him. He was the man Captain Hawke ordered to cut out my grandfather's tongue.

"Flame?" the King repeated, still touching my cheek. "That's quite an appropriate name for someone with such a hot temper. Tell me, Flame, is it true? You are pure... an untouched maiden? A virgin?"

I stood in silence, refusing to answer such a question, even if it was posed by my sovereign.

"She is," Captain Hawke answered, "I am sure. She's quite innocent and inexperienced, Sire."

Another soldier standing beside me kept shaking his head back and forth. King Shane stepped back, still staring at me, before glancing at the man.

"Something troubling you, soldier?"

The man nodded. "Your Grace, I must warn you. She told us she is a half-thing, And the man-beast took her before we captured him. No doubt he has already fucked her!"

Captain Hawke coughed, scowling at the soldier before turning to the King. "Sire, she tried to scare us with her claim. She's bluffing, nothing more. There's no proof she's a half-thing. And if you doubt her purity, you can test her yourself, Sire."

The King looked back at me, sizing me up and down with this new information. "You were with the man-beast? Did he pierce your cherry?"

I refused to answer.

"Captain Hawke," the King spoke in a decidedly perturbed manner. "You disappoint me. Must a common soldier be the one to tell me truths you choose to hide from your King?"

"Your Grace," the Captain replied. "Young Riley is new to our company and easily fooled. Pay no–"

"Enough!" King Shane bellowed. He turned to one of the other soldiers standing beside him. "Fetch the man-beast. Bring him here, and we'll see if he knows this flaming cunt."

The roaring bonfire provided the only warmth on this cold, clear winter afternoon. Standing in my linen gown and white leather thongs, I shivered against the chill. Thankfully, my grandfather standing nearby, remained wrapped in his wool blanket. He kept glancing at me with defeated, downcast eyes.

We all waited in silence for the 'man-beast.' I knew it must be Theron, but I wasn't sure how I would react to his presence after learning about the two fuck dolls he had taken. I stole a look at the covered wagon where two soldiers helped someone down to the ground.

It was Theron alright, his legs shackled in chains. Our eyes met briefly before I turned away.

One of the soldiers came running ahead of the other, slowly marching Theron toward us.

"Sire, the women, the two fuck dolls you gifted to him are gone!" the soldier announced.

"What?" the King cried. "How?"

As Theron got closer, he fixed his eyes on me.

*Flame. Use your powers. Run!*

I blinked, nodding my head. I did not want to hear his voice and certainly didn't want him to read my mind. But I could not quiet the questions filling my head.

*You took those women as gifts after you fucked them?*

Theron was shoved closer to the King. A soldier holding a cross-bow kept it pointed at Theron's head.

*Yes, Flame.*

I wanted to scream at his words echoing in my head. How could I have been so stupid, so naive, to give my heart away so quickly?

So stupidly?

"Theron!" The King boomed with anger. "What happened to your fuck dolls?"

"I set them free." Theron glanced at me, then hung his head.

"What? Why?" The King spat into the snow. "You had no right! I gave them to you to use for your pleasure. No one gives away a gift from the King!"

I watched Theron's face closely. He seemed to be in anguish. "They are not 'property,' Sire. They deserve to live with dignity and to marry if they so choose."

"Marry?" King Shane snorted. "A fuck doll marry? That's against our laws. They'll be stoned if they're caught running from their master."

"They have no master," Theron retorted.

"You disappoint me, man-beast, just like the Captain." the King said, glancing at Mason Hawke. "I was hoping one of you would have what it takes to become General of all my Guards, with a title and property and fuck dolls of your own. But I see now I can't trust either of you."

"Sire, I've always been loyal," Captain Hawke pleaded.

"Loyal to yourself, Hawke!" The King snapped and then turned toward Theron. "And you, man-beast? Will you bend the knee? Pledge fealty to me?"

*Never!*

I heard Theron's reply in my head, although he did not answer the King's question. There was a look of hurt in Theron's eyes. His thoughts filled my mind.

*I'm sorry, Flame. I do not deserve to be with you.*

The King seemed to take notice of the way Theron and I kept looking at each other. King Shane smiled—an evil, despicable smile. It was a countenance of contempt, surely nurtured by a life of spoiled privilege and a position of absolute authority over every other person in the Braeyork Dominion.

"Did he fuck you good, Flame?" the King asked in a lecherous tone, "with that big man-beast cock of his that filled Misty and Sasha's cunts while I watched him have his way with each of them?"

My hate for the King was countered only by my rage at Theron. The scene being described should not have provoked such jealousy for a man whom I had been with for but a few scant hours.

And yet, I was consumed by jealous rage.

"And you, Theron. Is that why you freed your fuck dolls? You want to be with Flame, don't you?"

The King had managed to disparage all who stood in the circle by the crackling bonfire. Theron said nothing, and Captain Hawke cowered beside him, a pathetic weakling who had lost favor with his King.

"I will give you a chance, Theron, to prove your worth and true character," the King announced. "You and Captain Hawke will do battle, a fight to the death. It will prove not only which one of you is most loyal to your King but also who is the most cunning and ruthless. Who is the one most worthy of being my General?"

"I will not fight," Theron replied.

"Then you've made the decision easy for me. I will have you and your beloved half-thing burned at the stake. After you watch me take her virgin cunt!"

My mouth dropped in fear. But I couldn't untangle the emotions running through me enough to concentrate the hatred I felt toward the King. I was too hurt and distraught by what Theron had done with those women.

Captain Hawke drew his sword. "Sire, let me prove my worth. I'll gladly fight the man-beast to the death. And if for some reason I do not prevail, my death will be in tribute to your long and glorious rule."

"Fine," the King replied. "If you manage to kill him, I may yet smile good fortune upon you." He turned toward the soldier with the cross-bow standing near Theron. "Unshackle the man-beast. I want to see him fight."

The soldier complied, and as he unlocked the shackles around Theron's ankles, King Shane offered a further incentive. "I will let Flame live, man-beast. But only if you kill the Captain and bend the knee to me."

*Never!*

I heard Theron's voice again as Captain Hawke rushed forward with his sword drawn toward Theron.

"Look out!" I cried.

Theron ducked in time to avoid the Captain's drawn sword. Hawke swung around quickly and began slashing his weapon back and forth, approaching Theron, who remained crouched on the ground.

*I will not fight!*

Theron's thoughts filled my mind. I felt his anger. He did not want to be drawn into a battle for the King's amusement. But I did not believe he wanted to die this afternoon.

"You're a pussy, aren't you?" the Captain shouted. "The King will get to try your Ginger whore, after I cut you down." Hawke kept swinging the sword back and forth, and still, Theron remained crouched, refusing to fight.

"What's wrong!" Hawke screamed. "Are you too drained from cumming all over the king's fuck dolls?"

The words burned my ears. I remained frozen in a combination of fear, confusion and rage. Theron's mind was a knot of emotions as well, and I couldn't unknot his feelings from mine. I did not want to hear his thoughts or experience his inner voice.

But still they filled my mind.

I tried not to stare, but when he glanced at me, I caught the red glow in his eyes and watched white fur cover his face. The more Hawke taunted, the more Theron transformed. The beast was taking control.

Finally, Hawke rushed at Theron, haunched and looking like he was ready to spring. In a flash of arms and legs, Theron seized the Captain. They rolled on the snow-covered ground. Hawke managed to spring free, still gripping his sword, as Theron lay on his back.

It would take but one strong thrust, and Hawke could drive the blade deep into Theron's chest. But as the Captain coiled his arm to attack, Theron knocked the sword out of Hawke's hand with a powerful kick.

Enraged, Hawke tried to jump onto Theron. But instead, Theron grabbed the Captain, flipped him over and pinned him down. Theron the man-beast, sat on Hawke, snarling at his prey.

Hawke cowered in fear as Theron growled and bared the sharp canine teeth extruding from his mouth. The growling, guttural noises from Theron were those of a full-grown Midnight Lupus male, an animal that could bring down the largest game in the forest. Like the big wolf who had hunted me in the forest, my mind connected with the beast inside Theron.

*Must kill him!*

Theron's wrath filled my mind. I hated the Captain, but I could not bear to watch this. Theron's lowered his head, opening his jaw as he pinned Hawke's shoulder to the ground.

"That's it, Theron!" the King screamed. "Finish him off! Take Captain Hawke's place by my side. Show me what you are made of, General Theron!"

Theron growled again and lowered his face to the Captain's neck. With his jaws stretched open wide, Theron hovered—growling, snorting, grunting.

"Please, no! No!" Hawke cried in a withering voice.

Theron hesitated. His shoulders sagged. He hung his head and spoke quietly. "I will not kill."

He pushed himself up and off of Hawke, who remained on his back, laying on the ground, staring at Theron, who took a few steps back and dropped to his knees on the snow.

Both men seemed to be in a daze.

"I said, to the *death!*" the King bellowed. "Hawke, now is the time to show me your strength. Do your duty, General Hawke!"

Captain Hawke, still looking confused, reached for his sword and raised himself up. With teetering steps, he approached Theron, still kneeling in the snow with his head drooped down.

As Hawke began to slowly raise his heavy sword, a screaming voice pierced the still afternoon air.

"Fire!"

We all turned in shock at the sight of the King's covered wagons consumed by the flames of a howling inferno.

# 16

## THERON

A soldier came running toward us as we stood stunned, watching fire consume the King's three covered wagons.

"We caught them!" he shouted breathlessly at King Shane, standing dumbfounded.

"Caught who?" the King retorted.

"Two women," the soldier replied. "Trying to run, still holding torches."

"Two women?" King Shane repeated. "Misty and Sasha, the fuck dolls I gave the man-beast?"

"Yes, we got them!"

The King bellowed. "Bring them to me!"

I watched as the flames continued to lick high in the distance. Most of the soldiers had run to try and save what they could of the wagons, but it was far too late for them to do anything more than get the horses to safety and throw shovels of snow at the raging blaze.

Flame stood in her linen robes, glancing at me before looking away. I focused my thoughts plainly.

*I am not worthy of you.*

She turned her head toward me. I couldn't read her staid face. Her thoughts were jumbled, difficult to discern.

The Captain stood with his sword drawn, but our battle was over. With the King's men occupied for the moment, we waited in the bright afternoon sun, uncertain of our next moves, as two soldiers escorted the women toward us.

Misty tried to run to me, but one of the soldiers grabbed her and threw her down at the feet of King Shane. Sasha, with her head down, stood near Misty lying in the snow.

"Why ladies?" the King asked, his tone harsh and vindictive. "Why would you do such a thing? Why did you betray me?"

"We feared for our master!" Misty replied. "We saw he was in trouble, that you were going to hurt him!"

"Your master?" the King repeated sarcastically. "I thought he freed you?"

"Yes, because he wants to be with his wife. He told us he could not be untrue to her."

The King turned to me. "You're married, man-beast?"

I shook my head.

Sasha glanced at Flame, who stood staring at the two former fuck dolls. "Sire, I think Misty is confused. He freed us because he told us no one should own us."

She paused a moment, looking over at Flame. "And that his heart was spoken for already. I believe he *is* married," she hesitated. "But only in his heart."

Flame looked at me curiously.

*Is that true?*

I wanted to respond, to tell her my life was worth nothing without her. If she could read my thoughts, I would not be able to hide my feelings.

"You are both stupid fuck dolls!" the King snorted. "So easily led to believe such romantic nonsense. I gave you a life of comfort. And this is how you repay me?"

"Sire, the fault is mine," I interjected. "Punish me for what they've done. I beg you, spare them."

The King laughed. "Spare them? Hardly! They are going to suffer for what they've done. I'll let my men use all their fuck holes one last time before I boil these two treacherous creatures in hot oil for destroying the King's property. And then what is left of their heads will be affixed to the highest pike in Braeyork."

"You fucking bastard!" Flame shouted at the King.

His lip curled as he snarled back at her. "You and your *husband* will be next! How dare you speak to your King in such a rude manner!"

"Shut up!" Flame screamed. "Shut your disgusting, fucking mouth!"

Flame's face grew dark with a fury that seemed to consume her.

She leaned forward, closed her eyes and struggled to move her arms, still bound behind her. I thought I could see her long red hair begin to smoke as if ready to burst into flames.

*Free my hands, Theron.*

The message startled me, but I moved quickly and untied the rope binding her hands.

"Don't touch her!" King Shane yelled at me.

"Quiet, you!" she rasped.

Flame raised her arms and pressed her two pointer fingers together, forming a prow with them. She pointed at the King as if she were about to vex him.

Without opening her eyes, she spoke in a thick, ominous tone. "Be silent, forever, you wicked ruler of Braeyork. No more shall you speak, all the rest of your sad, pathetic days."

And then the tips of her crimson hair sparked and burst into tiny flames. She dropped to the ground, and I hurried to douse her burning hair with clumps of snow.

The King also fell, gasping and gurgling. He began to convulse in wild jerking motions. After a few seconds, his eyes bulged, and he fell into the soot-covered ground by the bonfire.

Captain Hawke rushed to his side, dropping to his knees. "Sire, what happened? Are you wounded?"

The Captain managed to raise the King's head from the ground. His royal face was dotted with bits of ash and soot. Black streaks of melting snow ran down his cheeks. The King's mouth opened, and he looked as if he was about to scream again. But no sound emanated from his open mouth and wagging tongue.

He reached for his mouth, stuck out his tongue and tried to take hold of it.

"Sire, speak!" Captain Hawke urged the King.

The King pointed to his mouth and shook his head. He looked up and pointed a long, bony finger at Flame.

The Captain and the other soldiers, myself, as well as Misty and Sasha, all turned toward Flame. The tips of her hair were singed in black. The end of a few hairs smouldered.

"What have you done?" Hawke screamed at Flame. "You took his voice?"

I took a step closer and helped Flame to her feet. She was winded, trying to catch her breath. "No. He did that to himself."

"You *are* a half-thing!" Hawke shouted. "For this, you will…"

Flame raised her arms, forming her hands into a vexing prow once more, this time pointing at Captain Hawke. She closed her eyes, and he began to gasp, grabbing his neck. He wheezed loudly, fighting for breath.

"I suggest you not threaten her or anyone here, Captain," I said quietly, staring at Flame. She nodded at me and lowered her hands.

The Captain slowly removed his hands from his neck. He stood gasping like a wounded animal. Finally, he sighed. "Very well." Hawke turned to the King, then over at Misty and Sasha, still restrained by two soldiers.

"If I may suggest, Captain," I continued. "You could speak for the King, who it seems no longer has a voice of his own. If you release us, *all* of us, no further harm will come to you or to the King."

"Speak for the King?" Hawke repeated. He looked down at King Shane, still dazed, his face wet and defeated in humbled indignation. The King nodded.

"Indeed, I must now be the King's voice," the Captain announced. "And *no*, he will not release you–"

Flame raised her hands again into a prow. The Captain shrieked, holding his neck and fell to his knees, choking and gasping. "Tell...her," he gurgled, "to... stop... the King.... releases... you!"

I enjoyed watching Captain Hawke grovel before Flame, with the mute King Shane sitting helplessly in the sooty snow beside him.

Finally, I moved closer to Flame and slowly lowered her stiff arms that were still locked in a vexing prow.

"Let him go. It's over."

## 17

## FLAME

It was turning into quite an afternoon at the Painted Owl in the heart of tiny Dunfled village.

My grandfather Omar invited Theron and the two women Misty and Sasha, who had torched the King's wagons, to join us back at the Owl for food and refreshment.

And he also welcomed more than two dozen village towns-people and even one young soldier who deserted the King's Guard after the destruction of the camp. Together, we all crowded into the little pub and inn. Omar wanted to serve everyone, but Misty and Sasha refused to let him do all the work alone. They helped draw pints of fresh Dunfeld ale and tended the wood stove, warming meat pies in the kitchen.

I felt like I should help, and I went to see if I could lend a hand. It felt awkward to be alone with two of the King's former concubines. I could not quiet my mind, overflowing with questions about them and, in particular, about their time with Theron.

But Misty bubbled with infectious enthusiasm and insisted I sit and answer *her* questions. "You are so beautiful, mistress. I can't believe you are a witch!"

I smiled. "My mother was a Fae. And my father had Faerie blood from his mother."

"And your grandfather, Omar?" Sasha inquired. "Is he Fae?"

"No. He is the only one in my family who is not. He is all human."

Sasha sighed. "And quite a handsome human, to my eye."

We all chuckled, and then Misty touched my arm. "And you're the one, right? The woman Theron loves? The one I thought was his wife?"

Now, it was my turn to sigh. "I'm not his wife, and I'm not sure how –"

"He told me he could never be 'untrue' to you," Misty interrupted. "You are in his heart. I know it, and I can feel it in the way he spoke to us." She held a hand to her chest, staring at me intensely.

"Well, then," I bit my lip, "and I'm sorry if my words sound harsh, but if that is true, why did he fuck both of you?"

Sasha sat me down at the little table by the stove. "Because he had no choice. King Shane was going to give us to his men, to use for their pleasure, to fill all our fuck-holes, and then when they were done with us after a week, we were to be beheaded."

She lowered her head, her eyes wet. "Unless Theron complied with the King's request and fucked us as only a man-beast could while the King sat watching for his perverted amusement…"

Sasha sucked in a deep breath. "Unless Theron did exactly what the King demanded, Misty and I would both be dead after our bodies were grossly abused."

I sat in stunned silence.

"That is why Theron had no choice but to fuck us," Misty added. "But mistress, your husband, sorry, *your* Theron, he would not fill us with his cum seed. And I think I know why. That is something he will give only to *you*."

Sasha stood up and nodded. "And after we were gifted to him as his personal fuck dolls, he set us free. He could have used us in any way he chose. Instead, he gave us our freedom and told us he had great faith in us."

Before I could respond, my Grandfather burst into the room. "Ladies, we need those pies!"

After all the meat pies had been served, and everyone sat down to eat along with a frothy mug of dark ale parked in front, I took a seat across from Theron, sitting in the back of the pub, near where I had first set eyes upon him at the beginning of the week.

Everyone else in the Painted Owl was busy chatting. Sasha sat across from my grandfather, laughing as they slurped their ale and made short work of their meat pies. Misty fluttered around the room, filling empty mugs and no doubt catching the eye of more than a few men.

"I know what happened," I said quietly to Theron without looking directly at him. I concentrated on getting a fork into a chunk of beef in my steaming pie. I thought about Misty and Sasha.

*I'm ashamed of what I did with them, Flame. I will leave today.*

I laid my fork down and looked up at him. "Theron. You had no choice. You saved Misty and Sasha from being abused and beheaded. And then you set them free and told them how much you believed in them."

He raised his eyebrows in confusion. "How do know all –"

"Shhhhh" I touched his lips with my fingers. "And Misty thought we were married," I added with a smile.

He studied me as I kept my fingers pressed to his lips. Our eyes locked as my fingers touched his warm mouth.

*I don't deserve your affection, Flame.*

Was the beast side of his brain so primitive that he could not see I had forgiven him? He really didn't sense that I had put aside my doubts and now wanted but one thing?

*Theron, I am yours.*

He leaned closer, his eyes brightening. He took my hand, still touching his lips and began to kiss my fingers one at a time. I felt a longing deep within me, a need to finish what we had started a few nights ago in the hunting lodge.

I had to be alone with him, to give myself to the man *and* to the beast. Hearing my name spoken of as his 'wife' had warmed me and, dare I say, excited me so much that I squirmed with gnawing desire between my legs.

*I want to be your wife.*

He stopped kissing my hand and stared, his eyes glistening. He dropped my hand, bent low and leaned in close to me. I did the same until our faces touched. His words came to me with his warm breath upon my lips.

"More than anything else in this world, more than anything I ever desired, I want to be yours, Flame. Forever."

Our lips touched. It was not urgent or forceful but sublimely tender—as soft as the first blush of daybreak in the morning mist.

*Will you marry me, Flame?*

His words filled my mind like a thunderbolt from the gods above.

*Perhaps. But only if you ask me properly.*

Theron pulled back, grinning like a fool. He stepped up on his chair and raised his voice to get the attention of everyone in the Painted Owl.

"Ladies and gentlemen," he boomed, hushing all other conversations. "I would like to thank Omar for his hospitality today. And for the best ale and pies in all of Braeyork!"

This brought loud hoots and cheers. "And Omar, I would like to ask you for one other thing—permission to pose a question to your beautiful granddaughter."

Omar laughed. "Flame doesn't need my permission or my blessing for anything. But she has it, all the same."

Omar winked at me and then at Sasha sitting across from him. Everyone in the pub seemed to be smiling. Misty caught my eye and raised her eyebrows with a knowing look.

Theron jumped from the chair, bent down on one knee, and took my hand in his. "Flame, will you marry me and make me the happiest..." his eyes twinkled, "man creature in all the world?"

"Yes!" I shouted, pulling him up and hugging his bulging chest as tightly as I could manage. Everyone in the inn stood up and cheered. Misty was the first to congratulate us, followed by Omar, with Sasha trailing close behind.

"Welcome," Omar beamed, shaking Theron's hand vigorously. "Take good care of her, please. And try not to let her hair catch fire too often!"

~

Five long days and even longer nights later, the day of my wedding finally arrived.

Theron and I had found time to discuss a great many things. The difference, I suppose, from other betrothed couples was that we could do so without saying a word.

There would never be secrets between us.

We agreed we would avoid intimate contact until our wedding night. But each night, as I closed my eyes to sleep, my virgin ginger pussy, begged for attention. I resisted as much as possible but did give in the night before the wedding after a frank encounter earlier in the day with

Misty and Sasha, who were helping me sew a bridal dress and cut a veil of finely spun taffeta.

I stood before them, squeezed into the wedding gown, my breasts pushing against the tight constraints of the upper bodice. Likewise, my pinched thighs ached with the tightness of the girdle they insisted I wear. Once they had inspected and approved my ivory-colored bridal outfit, I happily changed into a simple skirt and blouse.

"Theron is a lucky man, mistress," Misty commented as I brushed my long red locks. She sorted through the dried flowers that would be used in my hair tomorrow. Without looking at me directly, she added in a sly voice. "And I presume you've never," she coughed, "been with a man?"

I nodded and replied sheepishly, "I am a virgin if that's what you are asking."

Sasha groaned. "Oh."

She sat cross-legged on the floor and looked up at me, combing my shining hair and over at Misty sorting through the flowers. "Flame, there is something you should know about your husband-to-be."

"I know, I know," I laughed, "he's a beast!"

We all giggled like children until Sashas stretched out her legs and then spoke more matronly and maturely. "I'm hoping you'll be able to... well, let's just say he is quite large."

She hesitated. "I could barely take all of him inside of me. His cock, when he is aroused, and the beast takes over, well, it is much, *much* bigger than any I've ever had before."

I had tried not to think about the fact that Theron had fucked both of them, and I had not asked for details, choosing to focus on the fact that it was only done to save them.

"I have seen his cock," I stammered, not used to talking so frankly. "I stroked it and made him cum... all over me." Speaking such words shocked me. But also excited me. I closed my legs to try and dull the damp longing between them.

"Mistress, listen carefully," Misty said as she laid down the dried flowers. "I also took all of Theron's cock inside my pussy, one inch at a time. He filled me like no one ever has before. You are going to feel a very sharp pain when he breaks your cherry, but if you can find a way to open yourself fully to him," she closed her eyes, "you will never want that cock to be anywhere else but deep inside you."

Hours later, I could not expel the memory of that conversation. And so, the night before my wedding, I played with my wet pussy and touched my excited clit. I made myself cum, muffling screams from my grandfather sleeping in the next room before I finally fell asleep contented, though still excited about tomorrow—my wedding day.

And... my wedding night.

# 18

## THERON

How I managed to make it through the whole day without losing myself to the beast within, I do not know.

My bride was the most angelic creature I had ever seen on this good earth. I felt deeply in love with her, and yet, with Flame's crimson and orange hair falling all around her virginal white wedding gown, I had to fight the growing bulge stiffening in my tight trousers as the day wore on.

The man and the wolf inside of me fought for control. I barely managed to keep the beast at bay.

She fit her wedding gown like she had been poured into it. Her pale breasts overflowed from the top of her bodice, and her wide hips flared from her narrow stomach within their silk confines as if to accent her fertility.

After the ceremony and the small reception, we were congratulated by all the guests before they left. Misty took a minute to whisper in my ear. "Be gentle with her tonight. She's a maiden still."

I nodded and fought to keep my bulging organ from revealing itself much more through my trousers. Finally, after everyone left, Flame and I found ourselves alone in the inn. Omar had given us the Painted Owl for our wedding night, including the two private upstairs chambers.

After the doors closed, Flame locked it and drew the shades. We had danced briefly as part of the ceremony, but now she wanted a proper first dance between husband and wife.

I took her in my arms and squeezed her tightly as we began to sway in a dance with very little forward movement. We moulded together as we moved, perhaps wishing to fuse our bodies into one. We had no need for words, yet Flame's voice filled my mind.

*I've dreamed of this moment, my love. I want you so bad. I am already so wet.*

I knew my wolf blood would soon take over if she kept this up.

*That is what I want, husband. The beast inside of you, inside of me. Please!*

I took hold of Flame's hips, grabbing her meaty ass cheeks and pulling her body into me. She ground herself against the outline of my stiff cock. I could feel my human side falling away. The wolf was consuming me.

White hair grew over my face. My fangs protruded, and I had an overwhelming desire to taste my mate for life. First, her lips and mouth, which she gave to me without reservation. I thrust my tongue into her mouth, fucking her with my long tongue until she almost gagged.

"Take all of me, Theron," she whispered when I finally released her. "I am yours now."

She took my hand and placed it between her legs. "This is your pussy. You own it."

I felt the soaking wetness through her silk gown. I needed to taste her, get my tongue inside her cunt hole and suck her hard clit. Dropping to my knees, I lifted her dress. She wore nothing underneath, and I almost exploded with the thrill of her seeing her naked pussy.

"You're my bitch," I moaned. I wanted to take my time to enjoy my wife for the first time. I stood up and stared at her. "Strip for me."

"No," she replied with a fiery look in her eyes. "Tear off my gown!"

If there was anything left of my human side, her command extinguished it.

I growled and, with a forceful tug, ripped open her wedding gown, revealing her full breasts, her smooth narrow waist, wide hips and her ginger pussy. She had shaved most of the hair, like Misty and Sasha. I grunted my approval, picked her up and carried her to the upstairs chamber, one of my thick fingers finding her wet opening and teasing her with each step.

Thick candles had already been lit, and I threw her onto our wedding bed, spread her legs and knelt between her.

"Has anyone ever licked you?"

"No," she moaned. "Except you, husband… in my most wicked and shameful dreams."

I growled my approval and spoke in a dark tone. "I'm going to make you my bitch. You're going to take my cock all night."

I tongued a path up her smooth legs to her waiting, quivering pussy lips. I teased the pouty petals guarding the opening. Curling my long tongue, I circled the wet entrance until she began to buck, groaning like a thing possessed, as she reached down and pulled my hair.

Her clit, poking out from under its little hood, begged for attention. I brushed her hand off my head. "I'm going to suck you so good, bitch!"

Her hands fisted into the sheets as I wrapped my arms around her thighs. I pulled her to me and clamped my lips around her swollen clit. My tongue played all around the bud, slowly teasing and circling it as my bride squirmed and cried, "suck me, please!"

Finally, I began to tongue her engorged clit. Slowly at first and then faster and faster. I moved one of my fingers to her pussy, outlining the wet entrance. I licked her clit until I felt her tremble.

"Fuccccccck!" she groaned, thrusting her thighs up. I kept licking her and pushing my finger inside the entrance to her wet cunt, around and around, stretching her open in preparation for something much bigger. She screamed and pressed my face against her pussy, leaving no room for me to move but instead just obey and devour.

My face was wet with her sweet pussy juice. I felt her cum once and then once again. She fell back onto the bed, shaking and spent.

I moved up on top of her. We kissed, letting her tears wash over us both.

# 19

## FLAME

We were not yet legally married. At least not in the eyes of the Braeyork Dominion. We would not be man and wife in the eyes of the law until after our 'first mating' was complete.

But to me, I was already his wife. Perhaps I had always been, and now I needed my husband the beast inside me more than I had ever needed anything in my life. He had pleasured me and made me cum better than I ever imagined possible.

But my empty pussy needed to be filled. And to be fucked as only the one who is put on this earth for you can truly fuck you.

"Let me see all of you," I whispered as he lay draped over my naked body.

He grinned, slid off the bed and started to undo the buttons of his ruffled white blouse. Slowly, one brass button at a time, he revealed his bulging chest, rippled with hard muscles covered in white hair.

"Oh my, husband," I cooed. "I've dreamed of you all week. I even made myself cum with my fingers, thinking about this moment."

Theron's smile was gone. It was replaced by a dark look of lust. I pinched my nipples as I watched him undo his leather belt and slide his trousers down. His cock sprang free, the engorged head leaking drops of his sticky cum seed.

"Is this what you want?"

"Yesssss..." I spoke the words in a far-away voice. "I need to be mated by the one who now owns me."

I stared at the massive size and girth of his hard cock. Dark purple veins ran the length of it, even around the thick knotted middle. Misty had taken all of it inside her, but she said Theron would not give her his seed. Such a privilege, she claimed, Theron would bestow only upon me. My pussy ached for that cock now, and I knew I could never be complete without his fuck seed deep in my womb.

Spreading my legs, I waited anxiously for him to climb up on top of the bed and mount me as his fuck thing, to take his wet cunt, the one he now owned. Silently, he moved onto the bed, grabbed my legs and spread them apart wide. My pussy was open, waiting, begging, to be filled for the first time.

His cock pulsed and jerked as he manoeuvred into position. He grunted as he rubbed the thick cock head up against the entrance to my anxious pussy. I was afraid of taking a cock for the first time, and yet, desperate to have him, my Theron, deep inside me.

*Breed me, husband.*

I knew he could read my thoughts. And I could read his. It was not only our bodies that could fuck.

He snarled as our eyes locked together.

*Yes, my fuck bitch.*

With a guttural moan, Theron moved the head of his cock against my wet cunt hole. He slid it around, working the slippery head over my engorged lips before sliding it under and over my clit. He did this a few times before slowly working the head of his cock into my waiting pussy.

*Never stop fucking me.*

I closed my eyes as the feeling overwhelmed me but quickly popped them open again. His eyes glowed red, and I knew he was now all beast. I could feel his desire, not only through his cock stretching me wider and wider but also within the depths of our shared minds.

The pain of being opened for the first time was excruciating. I trembled as he pushed in more and more of his hard organ, then relaxed, slowly pulled out and rubbed the head of his thick cock around my wet pussy lips again.

*I feel your pain, wife.*

"I have dreamed of feeling this," I whispered. "Open me!"

He smiled, and I smiled with him. This was our wedding night, the start of our life together. I needed to experience the agony of being taken by my husband for the first time. It was the pain of passion, a hurt making me feel truly alive.

"Fuck me!" I screamed like a crazed she-thing. "Fuck me hard!"

Theron pushed his monstrous cock into my cunt with one sure thrust. The pain exploded in my head. I knew he felt it too. We both screamed as his cock found its true home, deep inside my tight pussy.

I trembled with the sensation of being filled, stuffed with the impossibly large cock of a beast who now possessed me. Waves of pain knifed through my body, rippling through the walls of my pussy. A sharp ache reached deep inside my womb.

Theron shuddered as I wrapped my arms around him. I had taken all of him, but I wanted more.

*Use me!*

A menacing growl from Theron let me know he needed the same thing. His cock moved out a little, then a little more, until I felt warm liquid running down my legs. I was no longer a virgin, my blood proudly staining the sheets of our wedding bed. My aching pussy was now married.

*Now you will take all my cock, wife.*

My opened cunt needed it so badly. I screamed again as Theron pushed back inside me and started to ride me. He pounded into me, deep and hard. Our minds were one, transcending pleasure into the primal urge to mate.

I reached my hands wrapped around his back, clawing my nails into him. His furry chest brushed against my hard nipples as he slowed his thrusting. I could almost feel my pussy adapting to the feel and shape of his ribbed beast cock. Each time he buried it inside me and held it there momentarily, we were no longer two half-things.

It was impossible to separate where he ended and I started. His cock was a part of me, my pussy a part of him.

I needed his cum seed in the deepest reaches of me. His thrusts got deeper and more urgent. My hips rose to meet each one as his cock slid in and out of my soaking cunt. I was crazed with desire, screaming each time he pushed back into me, possessing every inch of me.

*Breed your bitch!*

The wooden bed groaned under the weight of our first mating as Theron ravaged me with a ferocity that both thrilled and terrified me. His loud grunts and my screams echoed through the tiny chamber and, no doubt, all of the Painted Owl Inn & Pub.

A wave of pleasure overtook the last vestige of pain from my torn cherry. I moaned with the anticipation of cumming on Theron's cock. I could feel him in my mind, his euphoria and the moment of release building like a tidal wave of need.

I began to lose control, my pussy tightening around his organ. His body stiffened and trembled.

"Agggghhhhh!"

We screamed in unison as Theron spasmed, over and over, howling like a creature consumed with each thrust. I kept cumming, too, until finally, I was spent and empty but filled with Theron's hot seed and his thick pulsing cock.

We lay panting and catching our breath for a few minutes. His cock remained hard inside of me. My only feeling was blissful satisfaction. I sensed as much in Theron.

I stroked his hair as we lay together, still locked in the afterglow of our first mating. My pussy ached with pleasure and pain.

"I love you, Flame," he whispered. "I think I always did, even before I met you. I knew you somehow, in my heart."

I sighed. "I dreamed about finding you, too," I touched his face. The white wolf hairs were beginning to recede, and my fingers grazed the soft flesh of his human face. "I just didn't know if I ever would."

He lifted his head and searched my eyes.

The wolf inside of him had taken me in lust. Now Theron, the man who had become my husband, seemed to want something more. "I will never be untrue to you, Flame. I would rather die than cause you grief. I want to grow old with you, no matter if our life be filled with rags or the finest silk. I will be happy as long as I am with you, through good times and bad."

I smiled as tears wet my eyes. "And I am yours, Theron. Now that your seed is inside me, and we are legally wed, I feel as if my life is only now truly blossoming—a flower bud that has, at last, found the sun's true warmth."

He wiped my tears and gently kissed me. He rolled over and lay beside me, naked on the bed. I closed my eyes as he lightly traced my face with his fingers, massaging my cheeks, the tip of my nose and then the outline of my lips until his fingers were wet with my spit.

*Let's never lose this feeling.*

I wasn't sure if the words were mine or his. Our minds were one.

His hands wandered over my naked body, lightly stroking my neck and shoulders. His touch warmed me. I was at peace with the world, content to just lay here in the glow of our love. We needed no words, both lost in the moment.

As he continued his massage, his fingers teased the sides of my breasts and then gently found the full globe, kneading them until I began to feel my passion returning. He sighed with me, in no hurry to rush things. He pinched both of my nipples. I felt them stiffen before he returned to massaging my breasts.

The room was growing warm with his touch when I remembered that Misty said she had prepared a wedding gift for us. We would find it in the chamber beside us, she explained. It was the room used for bathing and dressing.

"Theron," I whispered as he continued to squeeze my breasts and tease the nipples. "I think there is a surprise in the bathing chamber, something Misty wanted us to have tonight."

"Misty? Oh, really?" he laughed and sat up straight in the bed. I felt naked without his hand on my bare chest. As I lifted myself up, I noticed the white linen sheets had been bloodied.

"You're a woman now," Theron said as he took stock of the soiled bed and the dark, dried blood smeared high up on my thighs.

"Your woman, Theron." I felt proud but also a little embarrassed. "Go check the bathing chamber while I find clean linen for the bed."

S itting in the tub of warm soapy water was the closest thing I could imagine to the eternal afterlife, which I had heard about so often growing up.

"Ohhhhhh…yesssss," I sighed as Theron washed me.

His hands reached into the warm water in the narrow wooden tub, soaping my legs down to my toes before moving up between my legs. He smiled as his hands drew closer to my pussy and rubbed my thighs. I so hoped he would not stop.

"Sit up, Flame," he commanded. "Let me wash your backside."

Misty had drawn a tub of warm water for us, and Theron had heated it up even more with scalding water from the stove before he dissolved the bath balms of lavender oil and calendula flower petals that Misty left for us. No doubt she knew that after our first mating, I would need cleansing.

"You're a strong woman, Flame," Theron muttered as he washed my back. His big hands scooped up the warm, scented water and let it trickle down my neck and spine before he continued to 'wash' my back.

The touch of his fingers thrilled me with anticipation. He reached lower and lower. I wanted more and wondered if he would ever take me from behind, like the animals in the barnyard. Would he even dare take me in my ass?

*Someday, I might.*

I laughed. There could be no secrets between a husband and wife who could hear each other's thoughts.

*I hope someday is not too far off.*

He chuckled and continued to glide his hands over my back, teasing me by plunging down into the water and rubbing my ass cheeks, squeezing and kneading them before returning to my back.

I knew what he was doing, and I was about to protest when he moved around to the front of the bath barrel and began to soap my shoulders. He wandered over my breasts, paying special attention to my nipples and then down to my stomach toward my squeaky clean pussy.

*You're teasing me!*

He knew exactly how to keep me on the edge of desire. He alternated between massaging my breasts, pinching my nipples, and letting his hand drop down over my stomach, just above my pubic bone. His fingers lingered, then teased all around my pussy and clit before returning to my breasts.

I moaned as he massaged them, squeezing and pinching my nipples before returning to my pussy. I grabbed his hand finally and pushed it down.

"Make me cum again," I whispered.

Without replying, his fingers found the lips of my pussy. He touched all around them and then, with his other hand, grabbed my leg and slowly massaged closer and closer to my pouting pussy lips.

"Oh, yes," I groaned. With his thumb, he circled my clit and then pushed two long fingers into my pussy. He began to fuck my cunt, reaching in and curling his fingers and stroking deep inside my pussy.

I had never felt anything so wicked and pleasurable before.

*Let me hear you scream, wife!*

He stroked me gently and slowly. And then hard and fast. He alternated the rhythm, and the more I moaned, the more his pace quickened. His fingers fucked me so good as his thumb rubbed my clit.

*Make me cum good!*

He grunted, and I thought I could feel his fingers fatten inside my cunt. I was exciting him as much as he was me. He curled his fingers, touching the roof of my pussy. With the steady stroking of my clit a wave of pleasure enveloped me.

"I'm cumming! Oh fuck, yes!" I screamed as he kept up his torrid pace. My body began to convulse. I screamed ferociously as I started to explode in waves of pleasure.

I had never experienced anything like this before. I shook for almost a minute before he finally released his hand. My body went numb. Tears ran down my face as I looked at Theron, still kneeling before me like some holy mystical creature.

"Thank you," I whispered. Thank you sooooo much."

He nodded. "I felt you cum – in my mind."

We stared at each other. I panted, trying to catch my breath. "My turn," I said between breaths. "Let me take you in my mouth."

Theron grunted a deep, low growl of need, no doubt the need of the beast inside him.

"Stand up," I spoke in a firm voice. "Come closer."

Theron hesitated momentarily, then stood, removing the towel he had wrapped around him.

I got on my knees, still sitting in the warm water of the barrel tub. I wanted to taste the cock of my husband and swallow his cum.

I did not just want it. I craved it.

*Then you shall have your cock to suck.*

No secrets, I mused. We would never have to guess each other's needs.

He moved his fat cock close to my face. The beast was back. I slowly stroked the full length of his stiff shaft.

"Your cock needs to be sucked," I whispered, still stroking slowly, teasing him the way he had teased me. "It needs to cum in the mouth of your bitch."

Theron growled and reached for my head. "Suck me!"

He pulled me forward, and I opened my mouth. I kissed and licked the purple cock head, tongued under it, and finally, still holding it, took a little bit of it in my mouth.

*This is yours now.*

His cock had filled my cunt to bursting, but it felt even tighter in my mouth. I gagged, trying to take the full girth of it.

I let my jaw relax as his thick fingers gripped my hair but not forcing me any further than I wanted. My throat tightened around his cock as I took more in my mouth and realized in a moment of panic that he had complete control over me.

He could easily stuff his entire length down my throat until he found release.

Theron snarled, growling as I sucked, stroking what I couldn't get in my mouth as he used me for his pleasure. I was now his fuck doll.

*Yes, yes!*

Our thoughts intertwined. His cock throbbed, and I knew he was so close.

*Give me all your cum!*

He thrust his hips forward, his cock pulsing in the tightness of my throat as he began to spurt. I gagged on the warm liquid shooting into my mouth as he held my head in place, but I was determined to take all my powerful husband could give me.

His cum kept spurting, and I tried to swallow, but there was too much. Finally, he pulled out, cum dripping from my lips onto the top of my breasts, already glazed with perspiration.

Theron groaned as I shared a final wave of his pleasure echoing deep inside of me.

Our wedding night was truly one of wonder.

# 20

## THERON

We slept naked in each other's arms that night under the clean white linen sheets Flame had found after our time in the bathing chamber.

Misty had indeed given us a fine wedding present, and as I drifted off to sleep embracing my bride on our first night together as husband and wife, I was too tired even to dream.

And I had nothing left to dream about, even if I could.

In the morning, I awoke well after the first rays of the winter sun brightened the window slats of our upstairs chamber. It took me a moment to remember where I was, but as I gazed over at Flame, still asleep by my side, it all came rushing back.

I was in bed with my wife, a woman who barely understood all the magic that lived within her. She was also the most desirable woman I had ever met and the most lustful. She lay beside me, her long red hair splayed over my chest, her head resting on my arm after she wiggled away from me during the night.

We hadn't just fucked last night. We had become one, crazed not only with animal lust but with love that comes from experiencing another person's deepest needs and desires as if they were your own.

Because that's exactly what they were.

She stirred in bed as I studied her bright face.

"Morning," she smiled.

"Good morning."

I leaned forward and kissed her nose.

"Did it all really happen?" she whispered, closing her eyes. "Our wedding? Our wedding night, or was it all just a dream?"

I moved away a little. I wanted to see more of her. "Yes, Flame," I whispered, "it was all just a dream."

"Mmmmm," she moaned as I brought my finger to her lips. "It was the best dream ever."

She took my finger in her mouth and sucked it. I felt my cock stiffen as I moved closer and let her take more of my finger. I wanted to kiss her.

*Then kiss me.*

She released my finger and opened her mouth. My lips were upon hers in an instant. We kissed deeply, and though the passion was just as strong as last night, there was also tenderness in our embrace. We bit each other's lips, giggled and sighed as our bodies pressed together again.

*Make love to me.*

Her words surprised me. We had fucked like beasts last night. I had mated her, and she had sucked my cock better than anyone else ever had. But the storm had passed. We were more than the lust of our loins.

Flame pushed me down on the bed and massaged my face, eyes, mouth and neck. I sighed at the feelings she was bringing me as she hopped up on top of my chest.

"I want you," I whispered. "And I always will."

She nodded and moved her hips lower, sliding over my stomach. Her naked thighs slid over me until she was positioned over my stiffening cock. She started to moan a little, a happy, contented moan, as she rocked her thighs and took hold of my cock with her pussy lips.

As I slipped inside of her, I knew that if I died this very moment, I would die the happiest man who ever lived. She sat on me with the head of my cock fully inside of her. She purred.

*How did I ever live without you?*

I stared up at her as she impaled herself on me.

*I was not alive before you, Flame.*

My cock was almost all the way inside her pussy now. She dropped herself, taking the rest of me deep inside her. I reached for her hips and began to rock slowly up and down.

"Mmmmmm," she moaned. "Mmmmmm."

In my mind, I could feel her love, her desire. And I knew she felt mine. We rocked like this, pleasure rising and falling, teasing, edging, playing—our bodies taking what they wanted from each other.

We continued for a long time until I rolled her over and pinned her down on the bed without pulling out from her pussy. Our lovemaking was like nothing I had ever known. We had slowly worked each other up again, and now, as I thrust into her with calm, deliberate strength, we knew it was again time to mate.

*Breed me, Theron.*

I pushed into her deep and strong, holding my cock inside her, reaching for the depths of her womanhood.

*Faster! Harder!*

Flame's desire was in my head. It mixed with my lust, and soon I was fucking her like the beast I truly was... the beast who needed to mate.

In a frenzy of thrusts and screams, we both came as if we were not two half-things.

We were one whole thing.

When the room finally went quiet, long after we were both spent, we held onto each other, terrified that something so perfect couldn't possibly last forever.

~

We spent the whole day in the Painted Owl. Laughing, playing, singing, joking, teasing and feeding each other, talking long into the night before we fell asleep in each other's arms.

We awoke in the morning to the sound of heavy thuds. Someone was pounding on the inn's front door,

The real world had left us alone for almost two days, but now it had returned with noisy urgency.

I pulled on my trousers and shirt and hurried downstairs. The pounding continued until I finally pried open the door. The familiar face of young Lieutenant Riley greeted me with a stern look.

"Theron," he barked. "We need to talk."

I looked over at the small crowd behind him. A few other soldiers and Flame's grandfather, Omar, stood with Sasha a few feet behind him.

"May we come in?"

I looked over at Flame, scurrying down the stairs. "What is it?"

*I'm not sure. Trouble, I think.*

She took a few steps closer.

"Yes," I replied to Riley. "Come in. But this is Omar's establishment, so maybe you should ask –"

Lieutenant Riley pointed at Omar and Sasha. "Yes, I know. You and you too, please follow me."

Something was wrong, but I wasn't sure what to make of it. Riley escorted Omar and Sasha in the door, and then I caught sight of Misty running toward us.

"Misty!" I yelled.

"She should come in, too." Riley's tone was terse.

Misty ran in breathlessly, and the Lieutenant shut the door behind her. We all stood in a little group, no doubt wondering what Riley was doing back in Dunfeld.

"I have orders from King Shane to burn down this village and to behead both of you," he pointed to Flame and me. "I have also been ordered to escort the King's fuck-do..." he hesitated, "to escort Sasha and Misty back to Braeyork Castle."

*Why is he telling us this, Theron?*

I glanced over at Flame. Good question. I knew from serving in the King's Guard that actions of this type, orders from the King, were executed ruthlessly and without explanation to the hapless victims.

"Lieutenant Riley," I spoke, "why are you telling us this?"

"Theron," the Lieutenant replied, "the King has gone mad. Even worse than after he had his own stepmother beheaded to ensure his brother would never be born." He grimaced at his own foul words. "These new orders came from General Hawke, the King's voice, who has also taken leave of his senses."

"*General* Hawke?" Flame repeated.

"Yes, he believes *he* now rules Braeyork. The King no longer speaks—thanks to you." Riley glanced at Flame before turning back to me. "General Hawke issues all royal orders. Orders that I am no longer willing to accept. Orders that most of my men are loathed to obey."

Omar stepped forward. "Then why have you come?"

"There's great unrest across the Dominion," Riley replied. "I fear war is coming between the nobles. A new King might even ascend to the throne. But I cannot easily ignore a royal command."

I studied the young Lieutenant. I had not spent much time with him in my six months with the King's Guards, but I knew he was a thinking man. "Lieutenant, you haven't answered Omar's question. What's really going on here?"

Riley pounded a fist into his hand. "My men are split. Some are ready to burn down the town and do battle with you and your bride. But a group of us, we think you and…" he turned back to Flame, "and you. Well, you've inspired us. We would gladly follow you."

"Follow me?" I was confused.

"More calvary are headed here. If I fail to carry out the General's orders," Riley hesitated. "they–"

"Will complete them for you." I finished his thought and looked around at the little group.

"Yes! The two of you must run," Riley nodded. "Make your way to the Channel Islands of Highbridge if you can find safe passage across the Sea of Tenebrise."

We all stood in silence, absorbing Riley's news. He held my eyes a moment and then bent a knee and dropped before me.

"And if you permit it, Theron and Flame, we will join you. And we will swear allegiance to the noblest, most honorable and most powerful King and Queen the Braeyork Dominion could ever hope to find."

# 21

## FLAME

I reached for Theron's hand as Lieutenant Riley bowed his head down before us.

*Do you trust him?*

Theron nodded, catching my eye discreetly.

*Yes. He's a good man.*

"Lieutenant, I'm honored by your words, but I am no leader." Theron spoke firmly but with humility. "You are free to follow us if you feel it's not safe for us to stay in Dunfeld. I will fight *with* you to protect my wife if we are threatened. But I am not your King."

The Lieutenant stared up at Theron and then over at me. "You are more of a leader than you know. With your strength, humility and bravery, and with your Queen's powers, you could inspire a new generation all across Braeyork, a generation not driven by fear but of admiration for our Sovereign."

I stared at the sight of young Riley, still kneeling and staring earnestly at Theron. The King? And me, the Queen?

My grandfather stood nodding. "I swear my allegiance as well, King Theron." Omar dropped to one knee, "Sire."

Sasha and Misty followed the two men and bowed down in front of us. "Love live King Theron and his Queen, Flame," Misty swooned with a tone of reverence.

All of this kneeling and pledging made me uneasy. I just wanted to live in peace with my husband.

*And that is all we will ever need.*

Theron and I were happily of one mind.

I smiled at him. It was easy to see why Riley and the others would not hesitate to bend the knee and swear allegiance to him. The only Kings they had ever known were ruthless men to be feared. The thought of a King who inspired those around him seemed like a hopeless fantasy.

"Flame and I are honored with your faith in us. But we do not seek to rule Braeyork, only to live a life free of subjugation and cruelty," Theron said to the little group kneeling before him. "Please, stand up and cast aside your notions of what you think Flame and I might be to you."

Lieutenant Riley stood up. "Sire, time runs short. If you do not flee Dunfeld and seek the safety of the Highbridge Islands, I fear much bloodshed is at hand. Most of my men are with me and will follow you. But some will remain loyal to King Shane, and word will get back to the captain of the King's Calvary, who even now closes in on us."

*We must leave for the islands, Theron.*

Theron nodded after we exchanged knowing glances. I was beginning to realize how powerful it could be to communicate with my husband in this silent manner. I grinned for a second or two, thinking about how we would rule as King and Queen. Fairly and justly, I hoped, with the advantage of being able to read each other's minds and talk without words.

But I had never known a place other than Dunfeld. After my parents died when I was a young child, my grandfather raised me, and I had never gone more than a day or two without seeing Omar's loving face.

"Grandfather," I said as he stood up. "Come with us to Highbridge. I fear what will happen if you stay here."

Sasha stepped closer to him. He shook his head back and forth silently.

"She is right, Omar." Lieutenant Riley said. "My instructions were to burn Dunfeld, behead your granddaughter and her husband, and return Sasha and Misty to the King. I will not carry out those orders, but those who follow me will not hesitate to do so."

"I won't leave Dunfeld!" Omar spat on the floor. "I will fight if I have to, but this is my home." He turned toward me. "Flame, take the new King, your husband and make your way to the Channel Islands. You're our only hope for a better future."

"Grandfather, no! Please, come with us!"

My grandfather was a stubborn and proud man, but he couldn't fight the whole Calvary. And I worried what would become of him, alone without me helping him with the farm and the Painted Owl. We stood staring at each other in our little battle of wills.

"I will stay with you, Omar," Sasha broke the silence. "If you will permit me."

"Sasha," Riley spoke. "Not to be rude, but you were a fuck doll for the King, who still sees you as his property, even if he did give you to Theron. You must flee this place and make your way across the sea, or they will drag you back to Braeyork Castle."

Omar stepped forward. "Not if she is my wife!"

I gasped. "Your wife?"

Sasha took my grandfather's hand, beaming. "I would be honored, but how could we –"

"I will marry you," Lieutenant Riley interrupted. "Your name is no longer Sasha. Chop and dye your hair, dirty your face and keep to the barns until I can be sure the new King and Queen have departed safely."

Theron smiled. "Lieutenant, now it is my turn to be inspired. You have a good heart and a brave manner."

Stepping closer to my grandfather, Theron reached for Sasha's hand. "Sasha, please know that you are welcome to come with us to Highbridge. Or you can stay and fight with Omar and–"

"I want to stay!" Sasha cut off Theron in mid-sentence, "and fight!"

"As my wife?" Omar asked.

"Yes! Yes! Yes!"

I couldn't help but smile as she hugged my grandfather. There was something quite special between them, though many years of age separated the two. I giggled at the thought of Sasha as my 'grandmother.'

"Then it's settled," Lieutenant Riley announced. "Sire, I will have two of my men escort you and the Queen to the coast, where you can secure boarding for passage to the Channel Islands. I will stay here with Omar, Sasha, and the men loyal to me and send the others on a fool's errand into the Mortine Ravine."

The Lieutenant had already crowned Theron and me as the new King and Queen of Braeyork, but I wasn't in the mood to argue. I had to get ready to leave the only home I had ever known for a strange island with my new husband.

There was only one small detail left to sort out. "What about Misty?" I asked.

All eyes turned toward her. Theron addressed her in a gentle voice. "Misty?"

She bowed again as if he was the King of Braeyork, then rushed toward me and fell to her knees at my feet. "I will serve my Queen and King in whatever manner they so desire."

❧

I t had been exactly seven days since my wedding night, and now, on the fourth and final night aboard *The Braidfire,* we had settled into something of a routine.

The *'we'* consisted of Theron and I, along with Misty and two weathered and somewhat dreary-looking soldiers that Lieutenant Riley insisted accompany us across the open waters of the Sea of Tenebrise to Highbridge. Tomorrow, we would reach our destination after stopping yesterday at the Southern Atoll, the entrance to the vast string of cays, fjords, islands and bays that formed the Channel Islands named after the largest island in the group—Highbridge, our new home.

The two soldiers checked in with us twice a day but mostly kept to themselves as they scoured the three decks of *The Braidfire* for anyone who might have means or motive to threaten us. Theron and I believed that quite unlikely. Nor could we accept the Lieutenant's desire for us to assume the role of Sovereigns.

"When we get to Highbridge, we will sort this all out," Theron told me. "They may want a new King and Queen. But they will need to look elsewhere."

I agreed but had given up trying to stop Misty and the soldiers who insisted on addressing Theron as 'Your Grace" and me as 'Your Royal Highness.' Tonight, after our supper of salted beef, bread, butter and dried fruit, we retired to our cabins for one last night at sea.

The two soldiers bunked in on the lower decks with some of the ship's crew while we found a cabin for Theron, myself, and Misty. She slept on a small cot while we used a larger one covered in blankets and pillows.

Having Misty in the cabin for the last three nights had made any type of intimacy between Theron and me awkward. I knew from hearing his thoughts, and he certainly knew from mine, that we both ached at the forced abstinence.

I wondered if Theron felt any desire for Misty. He had fucked her, and she admitted that she had taken all of his massive cock inside her pussy. I tried not to think about them together and if he had made her cum the way he did me. She never spoke of it, but sometimes I noticed her stealing long glances at him, her mouth gaping open before she bit her lip.

As Misty removed her sweater and long skirt and crawled under the blankets of her small cot, only a few feet from our bed, I so wished I could be alone with Theron tonight. I needed more than just a polite goodnight kiss.

"Goodnight, your Grace," Misty sang as she blew out the last candle in our cabin. "And goodnight, my Queen. Pleasant dreams."

"Goodnight, Misty," Theron responded. "Sleep well. Tomorrow will be a big day."

"I will try, your Grace," Misty responded in the pitch-black darkness of the cabin.

I lay a moment, trying to ignore the yearning between my legs. I reached my hand to feel for Theron, and he grabbed my hand and started kissing it. I held back a squeal, squeezing my legs together with the desire building in my damp pussy.

*I want you so bad, too.*

Theron's words in my mind nearly made me gasp. He sucked my fingers, using his tongue on them the same way he did with my clit, teasing it back and forth. I moaned quietly. "Ohhhhhhhh."

Misty coughed. I froze, even as Theron kept teasing my finger. I tried to lay still but could hear Misty breathing so close to us and then heard her turn over in the cot.

*Shhhhhhh. Stop it!*

I knew Theron could read my mind, but he paid no attention. I pulled my wet fingers from his mouth, and he offered me his thick index finger, rubbing my lip and pulling it down. I was too full of desire to resist and hungrily sucked his finger. I wished it was his big cock he was feeding me, but I was happy to suck him however I could.

*I know what you want.*

His words thrilled me, even if we had to wait another night before it could happen.

*No. Tonight you will take the King's cock.*

I stopped sucking his finger and shook my head back and forth.

Misty was right there, a few feet beside us. I knew he heard every word I was thinking, but in response, he removed his finger from my mouth and moved his whole hand over my nightgown. He squeezed one of my breasts, massaging and kneading it until I could not help but moan. The more he squeezed, the more aroused I got, and when he moved to my other breast, I knew my pussy was already soaking wet.

"I'm going to fuck you," he whispered, placing his lips against mine, "hard and deep and long."

"No!" I rotated his head to face the cot where Misty lay.

*I don't care if she hears us fuck.*

Before I could protest, his hand dropped from my breast, slid down my stomach, and pulled up my nightgown. One of his fingers found my wet pussy. He shoved it inside me.

"Mmmmmmm," I groaned. Hopefully, Misty was already asleep. I prayed she would not hear us. Theron teased and finger fucked me before leaving my wet hole and circling my excited clit. I was going to cum if he kept this up much longer.

*I'm going to fuck you.*

Misty coughed again. This time I didn't care. I needed my husband's cock. We had never done it quietly, and I wasn't sure if we were capable of such a thing. I sensed the beast in him taking control. He removed his fingers from my clit, and I could feel him pulling at the sheets. He was undressing.

I spread my legs open.

*Fuck me good!*

He growled at my thoughts, and I was certain Misty knew what was happening. I thought I could hear her breathing but was too excited to care.

With much grunting, he positioned himself on the squeaky bed. I knew we were making a lot of noise. I reached down and took hold of Theron's cock as he positioned it at the opening of my wet pussy.

"Fuck your Queen," I whispered when he moved his mouth over me. "Use me!"

He growled and pushed the head of his cock into my gaping pussy. I cried out as he thrust deep into me. I reached around his back, scratching and clawing as he began to fuck me like he owned every inch of my wet cunt. I arched my back, my nipples pleading to be tasted.

*Take all the King's cock.*

We no longer cared that Misty lay but a few feet from us.

*Let's give her something to remember.*

I could almost see Theron's smile, and although I was a little shocked, I was also so wet and needy I did not care.

He stopped for a moment and whispered into my lips. "Shhhh, listen."

We both froze. And then I heard it too. It was Misty, whimpering, moaning and making little noises. She knew what we were doing, and she was no doubt pleasuring her pussy.

"Fuck me!" I whispered a little louder than before. "Fuck your wet bitch!"

Theron held my shoulders down and pushed back a little. His cock pulled out with him, almost exiting my sopping hole. Then he thrust back in hard, and we started to fuck like animals again, thrashing and moaning.

We could hear Misty's moans getting louder as we reached our moment of release.

"Fuck me!" I yelled as I sensed his cum about to shoot into me. "Cum inside your Queen!"

I screamed as Theron's cock exploded in my cunt, spurting his load deep onto the back of my fertile womb.

I heard Misty cry out, "My King!"

Then I lost all control and began to spasm over Theron's cock until I was spent. All three of us gasped and sighed loudly before the dark chamber went quiet once again.

# EPILOGUE

## FLAME

My smile widened as I counted Theron's steps while he slowly made his way up the inlaid stone staircase toward our little cottage on a bluff overlooking the Tenebrise Sea. It seemed like only yesterday we first navigated those mossy stairs, but it was, in fact, six months ago since we first stepped foot in Highbridge.

As he got closer, a familiar rush of feelings swept over me. Almost every night, our bodies and our minds united in a love that grew deeper with each passing week. We knew each other's needs and desires as if they were our own. When he gave me his seed almost every night, in my quivering pussy or my eager mouth, I came just as hard as he did.

It was not just our bodies that experienced exquisite pleasure. We felt each other's ecstasy in our minds.

Last night, though, was an exception. He was exhausted after returning home near midnight. Theron had worked a long day at the blacksmith shop alongside the proprietor to complete an order for fifty swords and shields for the Highbridge militia.

*I miss you.*

His words filled my mind as he finally saw me standing in the kitchen window. Those three words alone were enough to make me damp. I stroked the front of my material and thought about how he would fill me tonight.

*I want to taste you.*

He always knew exactly what I wanted, and the thought of his tongue on my clit, his fingers opening my pussy, and his cock in my mouth… I moaned, standing at the window, when a voice broke into my thoughts.

"Ma'am, supper is almost ready."

I had forgotten about Misty. She stood behind me, arching up on her tiptoes and looking over my shoulder as Theron approached the door.

"Thank you, Misty," I smiled awkwardly, hoping she hadn't overheard my moaning. "I think Theron loves that lamb stew almost as much as he does me."

"No ma'am," Misty giggled, "he's only a beast for you!"

I blushed at the innuendo. I often wondered how she felt about Theron and he about her, but I knew from his private thoughts she was not something he dwelled upon.

And although we were about the same age, Misty treated me with the respect normally reserved for someone much older.

Thankfully, she rarely called Theron and I 'Sire' or 'Your majesty,' though it was clear she still considered us her sovereigns.

Misty and I managed the cooking and cleaning, with most of my days spent tending to our little herd of sheep, pruning a sprawling patch of wild berries, and weeding the vegetable garden bursting with carrots, potatoes, beans and peas. I was glad to have her help but also thankful that she found a room in the village above an inn where she slept and worked most evenings.

The front door opened, and Theron stepped in. I greeted him with a wet kiss, lingering as long as I dared, with Misty watching us. If she hadn't been standing right there, I would be down on my knees, seeking out my husband's fat cock.

*After she leaves, my love, I'll feed it to your hungry mouth.*

I squirmed at the effect his lurid words had on my pussy, but managed to keep my composure.

"Evening, Misty," Theron smiled, glancing over at Misty, who curtsied before him. "Something smells *sooo* good!"

"We made the stew you like," she replied, smoothing her apron. "And the bread is almost ready too. I hope you like the way I made it, Sire."

Theron bowed his head. "I know I will, Misty. Thank you."

We ate dinner together, and it must have been obvious to Misty that Theron and I spent much of the meal in mental foreplay, smiling knowingly at each other as we exchanged lewd, teasing comments.

*My pussy is lonely.*

*And wet?*

*Soaking.*

As we flirted and tried to make small talk with Misty, she stared at Theron, only glancing my way when I addressed her directly.

"You're working tonight at the Inn?" I asked hopefully.

She hesitated before pulling her eyes off Theron and looking at me. "What?"

"At the Highbridge Inn—you're working there tonight?"

"Oh, yes, yes," she laid down her spoon and wiped her lips with her tongue. "After I help you clean up, I will be going."

"Misty," Theron spoke up. "I'm going to clean up tonight if you don't mind?"

"Of course, you are my…" she stumbled on her words, "my Grace, my Lord."

It was obvious to me that Misty was enamoured with Theron, perhaps seeing him as her King. But probably also as a man who had fucked her like no one else ever had and then released her from bondage.

When she finally left, Theron infuriated me by insisting on cleaning up the dishes before finally carrying me to bed, lifting up my skirt and burying his head between my legs.

As I felt his tongue on my clit and his fingers in my pussy, I knew that I belonged to him, and I always would.

And whatever happened, he would always be my King and I his Queen.

*The End*

# LEAVE A REVIEW!

If you enjoyed *Take by the Manbeast, The Legends of Braeyork, Book 2,* please consider leaving an honest review.

Your opinion matters to other readers searching for stories like this one - erotic romance set in a world of historical fantasy.

You can rate and leave a review on **Amazon.**

And you can also leave a review on **Goodreads** or **BookBub.**

Thank you so much for reading.

I hope you enjoyed the story!

# FREE SEQUEL - MISTY'S GIFT

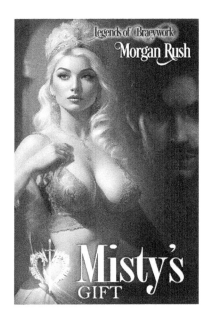

*Misty's Gift* is the novella-length sequel to *Taken by the Manbeast.* You can download FREE when you follow me as subscriber.

Please visit morganrush.com/subscribe to get your copy!

**Sold to the King**

*Legends of Braeyork, Book 1*

*Amazon, Kindle Unlimited, Paperback*

**Saved by the Warrior Wife**

*Legends of Braeyork, Book 3*

*Amazon, Kindle Unlimited, Paperback*

**Legends of Braeyork, Box Set #1**

*(Includes first three books and their sequels)*

*Amazon, Kindle Unlimited, Paperback*

## Dumped For a Sex Robot & Other Steamy Reads

*Book 1 of Hot Mess Short Stories*

*Amazon*

# ABOUT MORGAN RUSH

Morgan Rush writes timeless erotic romance set in a world long ago where magic has a habit of dripping from her pen.

She loves to watch *Game of Thrones* in pyjamas while getting her characters to fight to their last breath for their eventual happily after with benefits. And they do so enjoy the benefits!

Follow her on Amazon, Goodreads or BookBub or on social media for updates on new releases and special offers.

morganrush.com

# SAVED BY THE WARRIOR WIFE

## PREVIEW OF BOOK 3, LEGENDS OF BRAEYORK

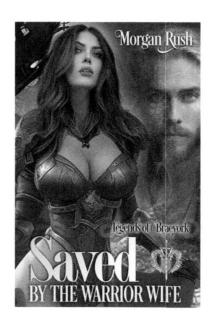

Chapters 1 and 2

# 1. SAVED BY THE WARRIOR WIFE

T hough I again questioned the reasons I had chosen to put myself in such a precarious situation, it was much too late to change my mind. I had no choice but to find means to keep from starving without being forced to sell my body.

Having acquired a position in Braeyork Castle under a cloak of deception, I stood listening to the urgent pleas emanating from the Prince's bedroom chamber.

Was it my place to interrupt such intimacy?

"Lia, please," the young Prince urged the chambermaid I was sent to retrieve. "Let me see all of you, the most beautiful woman I've ever known."

I had been given a task, and provided no one became wise to my deceit, I would do everything I could to fulfill the role I had accepted this morning as Prince Rolfe's temporary Squire. My long red hair was tucked inside a coif cap and then under a hooded cape chaperon, the uniform I was required to wear.

I carried a set of finely knitted hosen and braies, dark trousers, a crimson tunic and a starched white linen shirt – the ensemble I was instructed to dress the Prince in this morning.

I was uncertain how to proceed.

I stood in the drawing room outside his ornately decorated bedroom. Could I peek inside without being seen? The pleas from the bedroom were becoming urgent.

"Lia, I beg of you, as your Prince and as a man who loves you with my whole heart, please… allow me the privilege of touching your perfection."

Lia, the fair-haired chambermaid I had met for the first time yesterday, had not returned to the kitchen after taking up the Prince's breakfast through the servery. As he was expected to meet with the King and the High Meister this morning, I was sent to investigate Lia's tardiness and dress the Prince to ensure he arrived on time and presentably attired.

Holding my breath, I craned my neck and peered around the door. I bit my lip to keep from gasping.

The chambermaid lay prone and nearly naked on the Prince's ornate wooden bed inlaid with strands of gold and sapphire gemstones. Lia's blouse was open, and her breasts bared. Gathered around her ankles, her robe lay bunched, leaving her long legs and blonde womanhood exposed to the Prince's inspection.

He stood at the edge of the bed in his dressing gown, reaching for her thighs.

"You have always been my favorite, Lia," Prince Rolfe declared in a surprisingly husky voice for someone who had only recently celebrated his nineteenth birthday. "The maid I love the most, the maid who excites my senses, my entire being, more than any other I have ever met. You are truly an angel, Lia."

Shocked as I was at the scene, I could not avert my eyes.

Lia smiled, batting her piercing blue eyes at the Prince. Along with her long flaxen hair and milky white skin, her sculptured breasts and the silky tuft of blonde hair above her womanhood, I had to agree with the Prince's assessment – she was an angel.

"Your royal Highness," Lia whispered, "I'm but a simple chambermaid."

"Mmmmm," the Prince replied, his hand stroking the soft flesh of her thigh, "Not just a chambermaid, you are *my* chambermaid, Lia. I want to kiss you and your sweet, sweet pussy… as I do in my dreams almost every single night."

I held my mouth.

*Kiss her pussy?*

Was that a perversion of the royals? Though I had never heard anyone speak of this sort of intimacy, the thought of the Prince placing his mouth on Lia's most private parts excited me.

The room grew warmer as I watched. Lia's dark nipples stiffen, pointing toward the heavens. I touched my own tightly bound chest. My breasts, even larger than Lia's, strained against the coarse fabric I had used to bind them as part of my disguise. My nipples were surely as hard as hers.

I held a hand between the legs of my black breeches, hoping the growing dampness I felt would not be visible through the coarse blue fabric. I knew it was improper to spy on the Prince, yet I simply could not avert my eyes.

Squeezing my legs together, I scolded myself.

*Pantaka, leave. Now!*

But I chose to ignore my scolding.

"No one has ever kissed me there, your Highness," Lia whispered. "I think I would like that very much. Very much indeed, Sire."

She spread her legs open wide. I could see the moist lips of her pussy, the tiny petals of skin glistening in her excitement.

I kept my hand between my legs, gently rubbing my mound.

"Oh yes, Lia," Prince Rolf responded to her encouraging words, "I know you will enjoy it. I am going to use my tongue to make love to your pussy, and taste your little bud. I want you to cum all over my face, my dear sweet Lia."

*Oh my goodness!*

The Prince's words excited me as much as they no doubt did Lia. He opened the robe he had been wearing and threw it down, proudly exposing his physique. With his boyish good looks, innocent eyes, and the whitest teeth I had ever seen inside anyone's mouth, I couldn't help but gawk at his naked muscular body, broad shoulders and sculptured ass.

But what protruded stiffly from between his legs caused me to stare open-mouthed. I had seen a man's cock only once before, my brother's flaccid organ, as children bathing in the river.

This cock was nothing like my brother's. The Prince's organ was thick and stiff, the fat head naked of any foreskin. Lia's mouth hung open, the same as mine.

"Your Highness," she whispered. "I am waiting."

He fell to his knees and crawled toward her as she lay on the bed. He pushed her legs apart and used his tongue to trace a path up the inside of her thighs toward her quivering pussy.

Lia moaned as the Prince teased her, sliding his tongue all the way up her legs to the very edge of her wet womanhood, then quickly sliding downward and repeating the same action over and over until she groaned.

"Ohhhhhhh, your Highness. You tease me so good."

Could I watch this display of seduction without sliding my hand down the front of my own trousers? I badly needed to touch myself as the Prince pushed his head between Lia's legs and licked around the opening of her pussy.

She moaned softly, reaching down and tugging at his long sandy brown hair, grinding herself into his face. The Prince responded by wrapping his arms around her legs, yanking her closer and pushing her thighs further apart to fit his shoulders. His tanned fingers kneaded the pale skin of her thighs as he worked his head between her legs.

"You taste like lavender honey," the Prince murmured as he tongued Lia's pussy.

Both the Prince and Lia were consumed with lust. I crept closer, stepping into the bedroom. Neither noticed me staring. I knew my own pussy was soaking wet. It took all of my willpower to stop from pleasuring myself as I watched them.

Prince Rolfe seemed an experienced lover. His head moved from side to side, and the stiff cock between his legs bobbed up and down as he licked Lia's pussy.

"Oh, your Highness!" she screamed. "Please, suck me, Sire!"

The Prince grunted his approval, and I squeezed my legs together, imagining what Lia must be experiencing. He licked as though possessed by a demon, and she began to moan and buck. The Prince slid two fingers into her pussy as he licked her tiny bud. He lapped at her flesh with noisy abandon as his fingers moved inside of her.

Lia's moans became louder, more intense, and I felt my own excitement rising. She cried out, and I shuddered with a muffled moan.

As the Prince continued to fuck Lia with his thick fingers, his head moving back and forth over her bud, she screamed again, and I felt my excitement cresting in a wave of intense pleasure. I pushed my hand inside my trousers, my fingers gliding over wet skin and traced a circle where I most needed it -- my begging clit.

"Oh! fuck!" Lia moaned. "Please, don't stop!"

The Prince kept his frantic pace with both his fingers and his mouth until Lia screeched.

I screamed with her as we climaxed in the same glorious moment.

## 2. SAVED BY THE WARRIOR WIFE

### PRINCE ROLFE

I was so possessed with lust for Lia and so overcome with how hard she had cum from my tongue and finger fucking, that it took a moment for me to realize there was someone else in my room.

Snapping my head around, I stared in horror at a young man on his knees, his hands inside his trousers. His flushed face stared back at me with wide emerald eyes. A pinkish tone skated up his neck.

"Are you the new Squire?" I asked with the sweetly pungent taste of Lia's pussy on my lips. I glanced over at her as she pulled a linen sheet over her nakedness.

"Um," the man seemed as embarrassed as I was with the situation. Had he been rubbing his cock while he watched Lia and me?

"Yes, Sire, um… your Highness," the man finally stumbled in a halting gravel voice. "I am replacing Squire Odell until he has recovered from his illness."

"Oh, I see," I replied, taking a moment to consider this moustached man. I knew Odell was unwell, and frankly, I welcomed the opportunity to have a Squire closer in age to me. "I trust you are a discreet sort of fellow?"

The poor Squire nodded but looked disoriented as he straightened his uniform and rose to his feet. What a big lad! He was as tall as I, at over six feet. He was curious looking – the smooth face of a boy accented by a thick moustache and a bulging broad chest. And obviously, a lusty sort of man, much like me.

"Yes, your Highness. I am *very* discreet," he replied.

His eyes flashed over to Lia. She looked uncomfortable with the new Squire in the room and me standing there naked, brandishing a still-hard cock. But as Heir to the throne of the Braeyork Dominion, I was not overly concerned about either of them.

"Thank you," I hesitated, grappling for the man's name, "Squire…"

"Pratt," he replied. "Your Highness, I'm here to dress you. The King and the High Meister await your arrival. And Lia, you are to–"

"She's not going anywhere," I interrupted. "Not yet."

I wondered if I could trust this new Squire. Although I was the Prince of Crasmere and first in line to the throne, I did not want my private affairs becoming the subject of castle gossip.

The truth was I loved Lia. I know it was foolhardy and that I could never be with her. Still, I had dreamed of her for so long, cumming almost every night to the thought of her beautiful face and perfect body. She had been my chambermaid for nearly two years, and today, at last, I had finally revealed my feelings to her.

"Would you mind, Pratt? Give me a few more minutes with Lia, and then you can help me dress."

Pratt bowed his head. "Of course, your Highness. I will remain outside your apartment until you…" he stole a glance at Lia, "are ready to be dressed."

"Just wait in the drawing room, Pratt. And thank you."

As he turned and walked away, I cursed my foolish heart. It was my weakness, and I happily followed its demands rather than listen to my more sensible head. I would rather love Lia, than fuck all the shapely concubines my father always pleaded with me to try.

The moment Squire Pratt exited my chamber, Lia scrambled from the bed, and I wrapped her in my arms. We held each other, still both naked.

"I love you so much, Lia," I whispered into her shoulder, aching with my hard need for her.

"Your Highness," she replied softly, her breath warm on my lips. "You are soon to choose a first wife, to be betrothed. And I am married."

I held her tightly. My stiff cock pushed between her thighs as I reached around her and pulled her closer, squeezing and caressing her bare buttocks.

"I want you so," I whispered. "I am not whole without you."

Lia smiled and pressed her lips against mine, opening her mouth to me. I explored it with my tongue, grinding into her with my throbbing cock squeezed between her legs. Though nestled tightly, it glided smoothly across her slicked skin.

She pulled back and touched my lip with her finger. "Your Highness, only my husband takes my pussy. But will you allow me to taste you?"

Her denial crushed me, but the thought of her wet mouth wrapped around my pulsing cock was a thrill all the same. "Yes, my love, please. I will challenge your husband someday and claim you as my own."

Lia smiled and shushed me with her fingers.

Then slowly, she dropped to her knees. I looked down at her long blonde hair and the face of my wet dreams. She positioned herself directly in front of my twitching cock and took hold of the thick shaft.

"I know how much you love me, your Highness," she purred. "And I, too, think about you. But since my pussy is claimed, this is the only way I can show you my true feelings, Sire."

Lia stroked my bulging cock. "You are so much bigger than my husband," she whispered. "My little cunt is wet just thinking about sucking you, making you cum inside my married mouth."

Her words alone were almost enough to make me explode. A drop of cum oozed from the tip of my cock, and she eagerly lapped it up.

"Take me in your mouth, Lia, my love. Please!"

"Mmmmmm," she cooed, licking all around the slick head, wet from her licking off my first drop of cum. She opened her mouth wide and thrust her face forward, taking the entire head of my cock.

The feeling was unlike anything I had ever felt, even from the couple of fuck-dolls that I reluctantly allowed to service me. Lia's mouth was warm and inviting, her tongue soft, and she allowed me to shove most of my long cock into her as lust overtook me.

My fingers reached for her head, gripping her hair and forcing her mouth downward as my hips pushed forward. With one hand still gripping the base of my shaft, her other wrapped around my thigh as her nails dug lightly into my skin.

～

Thrust into her mouth, I groaned. "Take my seed, Lia."

She nodded as I began to pump in and out, my load rising quickly. I began to spurt, holding her head in place while I filled her mouth with hot cum.

"Ohhhhhhhh! Lia!" I shouted, trembling as I spasmed, then slowly released my grip on her head. She kept sucking as I spurted until her mouth overflowed.

Finally, she pulled back, cum dripping from her lips down onto her smooth chin and falling onto her pale heaving breasts. I fell to my knees, crying from the joy of finally taking me between those pretty pink wet lips I had dreamed of for so long.

"I love you, Lia."

She touched my wet face. "Your Highness, I will always treasure you and your feelings. You are so young, and I am sorry that I am…"

Without finishing her sentence, she stood up, quickly collected her uniform, and dashed from my chamber.

Watching her leave, still trembling from the release of my pent-up love, I rose to my feet, wondering if I would ever see her again. I stared at the door a few moments and then remembered the new Squire, that young fellow Pratt.

Had he been standing outside my chamber, listening the whole time?

Printed in Great Britain
by Amazon

40043911R00111